STORM-DRAGON

DAVE FREER

RACONTEUR PRESS

Published by Raconteur Press, LLC
production@raconteurpress.com
www.raconteurpress.com

Cover Design and Illustrations by Cedar Sanderson
Edited by D. Jason Fleming
Copy-edited by Laura Begley

CONTENTS

Chapter 1 — 1

Chapter 2 — 17

Chapter 3 — 27

Chapter 4 — 35

Chapter 5 — 47

Chapter 6 — 63

Chapter 7 — 73

Chapter 8 — 83

Chapter 9 — 91

Chapter 10 — 99

Chapter 11 — 107

Chapter 12 — 115

Chapter 13 — 127

Chapter 14 — 135

Chapter 15 — 147

Chapter 16 — 159

Chapter 17 — 171

Chapter 18 — 179

Chapter 19 — 187

Chapter 20 — 199

Chapter 21 — 209

Chapter 22 — 217

Epilogue — 227

Also from Raconteur Press! — 235

Also by Dave Freer — 237

Please, Tip Your Authors! — 239

To Molly the magpie and Peanut the squirrel

Author's notes on the universe of STORM-DRAGON.

This story is set in a future universe where the frontier between man and the unknown is close and vast. Faster-than-light travel exists. Humans have spread to and colonized many strange worlds. So far, no intelligent aliens have been encountered, but that could change tomorrow.

Earth—the source of most advanced technology, has—after a failed attempt to control the colonies, resisted by the Confederated Worlds—withdrawn into itself and cut them off, in an attempt to bring the colonies to heel.

The colonies don't care. Technology has slipped back a bit, but they have not gone crawling back to Earth rule. Colonists, frontiersmen, have bigger problems—like staying alive and building homes on new worlds, such as Vann's World, where this story is set.

Vann's World is younger, geologically, than Earth, with more water. It's a wild, terrifying, exciting world of volcanoes, and huge storms that make hurricanes look pleasant—especially around the equator. It has three moons, so enormous tides, and it is just bursting with life—where everything tries to eat everything else, in its fertile seas and across hundreds of chains of volcanic islands, forming and eroding away. Close to the pole, in the volcanically quietest area, is the Bering archipelago. Settlers came to farm here, on a seven hundred mile chain of thousands of islands. Every island is encircled by a sponge-like layer of coralline. Exposed at low tide this forms the first tier, a wide, mostly flat layer up to a mile wide, around the islands (helping to break the force of the waves). Every pool hides strange and deadly creatures, and when the tide rushes across it, so do the predators.

Inside that, is the second tier forest—on the rock of the island itself, like a vast mangrove swamp with the tangled roots trapping the tide-water and washed down nutrients—the root-dams are muddy and full of life, some of it dangerous, all of it hungry, full of traps for the unwary. The 'trees' are not mangroves though—they're a form of seaweed that absorbs water with the incoming tide to lift the branches and leaves and fruits above the creatures coming in with the tide, to protect them. Think of it like a bouncy castle where the 'trees' slowly deflate at low tide and then inflate again at high tide. The very high tide spills a little beyond the forest, when the third moon adds its attraction. Above that, the land is relatively safe. There are no trees, just grass-like plants and thickets of 'willow-withy'—dense and woody but flexible plants, about a half inch wide, and up to eight feet high. It's here our settlers made their homes...until the recent Ghat-Confederated Worlds' war.

The War seems over...

ONE

A savage wind, full of icy shards, bit at Skut's face around the edge of his parka hood. It kept him looking down, and not around, which was always a mistake on Vann's World. He would never have got that close to the diving hamerkops if he hadn't been trying to pull his head into his parka like a turtle.

He might never have heard the squall for *help!* Well, 'heard' was the wrong word. He felt it in his head...and it wasn't so much the word 'help' as the need for it.

"I'm coming," he yelled, which would have been pretty dumb even if the wind hadn't whipped the words away, because one really didn't want to make oneself obvious on the coralline spike flats. Too many things might notice.

But something did hear. And the *quick!* wasn't so much a word either, but a desperate need.

He saw the little electrical flash just before he saw the diving Hamerkop. All his father's training of him, meant he didn't even think, he just drew and fired his flechette. The dive ended in a splat onto the etched rock. The second savage bird managed to turn its attack on him, but he was still quick enough or lucky enough, to hit one wing and send it spiralling into a tide-pool, where it ended in a sudden snap of waiting teeth. That pool must have a resident slake-eel. Lucky he hadn't stepped into it.

The rest of the hamerkop fair, shrieking in rage loud enough to be heard even above the wind, held off.

Up against the coralline spike, with several blackened streaks around it, sat the most miserable little thing Skut had ever seen. It was *cold,* *scared,* and *HUNGRY!*

He picked it up without even thinking about it. It was maybe eight inches long, two thirds of that tail, and it curled into his palm easily enough.

Warm!

And then it bit him!

"Ouch! You filthy little beast!" Only the fact that it was clinging to his hand with all its claws and with the tail wrapped around his wrist stopped Skut from flinging it away.

Hungry! somehow that 'hungry' conveyed "food or die" to Skut.

"Well you can't eat me."

Somehow Skut got the idea that the miserable scrap of fur and tail was not sure just what 'me' was. And it was chewing the little bite it had taken. It was a very little bite, for all that it was sore. The little thing only had a tiny mouth. *Need food. Foood!*

Skut grabbed the fallen Hamerkop. The flechette needles had torn one leg nearly off, so he was able to pull the meaty drumstick free and put it in front of the little creature on his hand. "Eat that, not me. Now where can I put you?"

Warm.

Skut didn't know quite where that came from. The little beast's snout was already buried in the meat, the little tail still locked around his hand, as it gorged. But wherever 'warm' was, it wouldn't be here. The tide was going to surge over these flats, ripping through the coralline spikes pretty soon.

He knew he should just put it down and let nature take its course. The Hamerkops were higher, but still circling. That was what he was supposed to do. He also knew he wasn't going to. Somehow trust and contentment were coming from the little creature. He didn't even know what it was. His hand throbbed from the bite, but he still wasn't going to put it down. No, he'd head for high ground, and then he'd decide what to do with it.

Skut made his way carefully, because, well, Vann's World. It was a good place to end up being bitten or stung if not eaten by wildlife—and not just by tiny little things either. There was a second-tier shelf a little way back. They'd be safer there, even if it was harder going, with the plants. Mostly safer, anyway. Only some of the plants wanted to eat you, and some of the creatures living among them only ate plants. The sea was the real danger, this low down the tide-line, and the tide, he could see, was coming in fast.

He found a break in the first-tier cliff that he negotiated with one hand, just in time, as foamy ripples were licking at his heels, dancing with glass-fish. He scrambled up into the shadowy tangle of the second-tide tier. The little creature in his hand...burped thunderously.

"You should at least say 'excuse me,'" said Skut, grinning at the volume that had come out of the little thing.

Scuse me? with a faint air of puzzlement, and, with that, pushed its way under the elasticated parka cuff and up his sleeve.

"Hey!"

Warm. That somehow conveyed contentment, and sleepiness.

Well, it gave him two free hands and he'd need them. The second-tier forest was at the floppy stage as it always was, just before the tide made it into the tangled root-dams. The vegetation tried to trap the water, but by the time that first tide started flooding, most of it was gone. Earlier on the tide you could move easily enough through the forest, as long as you root-hopped. Now you had to push past drooping branches, heavy, slightly soggy spongey things. Even the snapper-leaves were flaccid, and the stinger-vines drooped. One still had to avoid them, but they didn't swing after him. The lurkers in the root-pools were waiting for the flood and the food it brought. All he had to do was get through, scramble up to the third-tide tier, and he could sort himself out.

He could work out what he was going to do. Two hours ago, running away from Highpoint Station had seemed a good idea. Actually, the only idea. He wasn't allowed to hit them. They all hated him and...and how else could he deal with the situation?

Only, he hadn't really thought about where he was going to go or...the practical things. He'd just wanted to be away from Highpoint Station, away from school. Ideally, back on Faraway where no one bothered him.

But that wasn't going to happen. Home—Faraway Station—was more than three hundred miles away, at the far end of the Bering archipelago. Thousands of islands, some joined up at low tide, some with deep channels, between him and what would always be home. Stuck here, where they hated him.

Then, pushing through the last layer of fronds, he realized he was stuck right here, let alone on Highpoint Station. Highpoint wasn't really very high, but the cliff in front of him was. It was actually only about twenty feet, but it overhung, making a shallow sort of cave along the bottom. He had maybe half an hour before the rising tide made it a deep-water cave. Cold water too at this time of year, but still swarming with little fish, being chased by bigger fish, and being chased by even bigger fish, all staying safe from the fish that were too big to come into the shallows of the second-tide tier forest.

Skut began to jog along the cliff line, hoping for a break in it. He hadn't been running for long when he felt a squirm and the little creature moving up his sleeve to his shoulder and neck. He just had to hope it wouldn't bite him. He didn't have time to stop and try to get it out now. There'd been one of the spring storms this morning, which would make the surf coming in big and wild.

And sure enough, he heard the strange creaking, groaning noise on the wind, along with the distant roar of the waves. The first of the second-tier trees were getting water flooding around their roots, sucking it in and expanding, standing tall again. That meant he had maybe ten or fifteen minutes before the water got to his feet. The cliff looked unbroken, so far.

He was in deadly trouble. This was why they didn't let the people in Highpoint Station out to wander around the island. He'd hated that, and now it might just kill him. He looked, as he ran, for a flaccid tree he could climb that might take him close enough and high enough, when it expanded with the flood, to make it possible to jump to the top of the cliff. It was a little lower here, but even more overhanging, with the trees further back. Then he realized he could see a far wall. This was like a gorge or something.

A few hundred yards and he knew he was right: it was a gorge. He was about to turn around and run back—too late, when he realised what it was—a drainage gorge from the next tier. And yes, there were the pock-mark holes of the bristle-worms that would fill the gorge with a web of feeding bristles, ready to spear any prey carried through by the water—rising or falling. He ran a little faster, panting now, pushing back his parka-hood, wishing he had time to unzip the jacket properly. Up, up into the narrowing throat, the overhanging walls closing over him, the bristle-worm burrows in the rock closer and closer together, little spear-spikes sticking out. He had to be really careful not to touch them and he had to hope the throat didn't get too narrow. It hadn't so far, but the floor of the cave was crunchy with fallen fish bones. The bristle-worms would spear them, pull the harpoon-like little spear back in, pulling their prey against the wall, and feed on it.

Behind him the forest was standing up, which also meant the waves could come through faster...and harder. He could hear the crunch of the first wave hitting the cliff. It would be funnelled up here, and in a fairly short time this gorge would be a squirting blow-hole. A running spill-deer came rushing past him. Any animals that didn't want to swim but had gone down to feed in the second-tier forest, had to either fly or run up this way. But a spill-deer wouldn't do him any harm...

It was only when he saw the daylight at the opening of the throat, and heard the gurgling growl of the Loor-beast standing over the body of the spill-deer that he realized that this would make a perfect hunting place for the huge predator of the upper tier.

He was in a world of trouble. Behind him the next wave boomed, spray laden wind hitting him in the back. In front of him the Loor opened its long, wide mouth, all snaggled teeth and meaty breath. Even though he had the flechette pistol in hand, Skut knew real terror. They were just so big, the skin so tough, and he had nowhere to retreat to. "Oh, help!"

Help! Darting out from his parka, a blue and white fluffy arrow hurtled at the Loor beast on little wings, riding the spray-laden air. It paused just above the Loor's jaw. The creature snapped at it as the fluffy fur flared out, making it look twice as big. It still wasn't very big. Then there was snap and a fat blue spark leaped from the little creature's long tail, to the Loor's dripping mouth.

The predator gave a startled yelp, and snapped its mouth shut. It must have got nearly as big a fright as Skut had, as it took off running. Skut would have run too, except that, as he turned the spray from the funnel hit his face, and he could see all the little bristle-worm spears emerging. And the little fluffy winged thing landed clumsily on his shoulder with a sharp smell of ozone, and *I am pleased with myself* feeling. And...*hungry* (not starving, like last time, but like, 'that took some energy, and I want food'). And then, distinctly, in his mind *'scuse me.*

Scut's mouth fell open. It was trying to talk to him! The

rest had been, well, feelings. He holstered his flechette, trying to process it all. Another wave boomed into the funnel. Thinking could wait. The Loor might easily come back for its prey, and a spout of water certainly would! He started moving off, hastily, but was interrupted by a fierce *hungry.*

Obedient to the command, he used his belt-knife to cut a strip of flesh from the ripped open belly of the spill-deer, and then, with meat in hand, took off for any place else. It was—other than a few big predators like the Loor, probably safer than anywhere but the land above the high-water line. That was where he was heading. Not a lot of Vann's World's creatures went where the tidal flood didn't reach. Spill-deer, Patratti, birds...not like the lower tiers.

The little lithe furry thing climbed down his arm and reached for the meat. "Hey. Don't make holes or get blood on my parka. Mom would be mad with me."

Obediently it used its long tail instead. It understood. Well, understood something. *Mom. Fur.* It hung like a bag from his hand with the strip of meat and ate. Skut found a rock a few hundred yards from the blow-hole gorge, and sat down. "Rock at your back, clear field of fire," he muttered. Papa's first rule for a rest. Either someone or a rock behind you. What was he going to do?

He had got through trying to survive his own stupidity, to being miserable again. But not quite as miserable, not quite as head-down-and-run, as he had been. Being on the wrong side of an angry Loor did make having his trousers split when he bent down, in front of all of the other kids, less bad. His face flushed with the memory of it, and that... Hillary and her friends mocking his undies. That was on a par with the Loor. They had been white! They had just got washed with Papa's red sea-kit.

"Mrreeep?" said the little fur-strip leaving its gory feast and coming up to touch his face, along with something that could be best understood as *What nasty?*

It tickled a bit. "Not you, little beast," he said smiling, despite all his upset and worry, and, without even thinking about it, began stroking the creature. It suddenly occurred to him that a lot of Vann's World's creatures had toxic spines and other surprises...well, too late. It had been on his hand and up his sleeve, and out his neck and now was rubbing against his face. Somehow, it radiated *content* and then *scuse me!* and burped. Skut had to laugh. "But you're a problem, to add to my other problems. Just what do I do with you?" Somehow, he knew it was basically just a baby. If he left it here, it would die. Yes, it appeared to be able to deliver electric shocks, but he was pretty sure that it couldn't feed itself.

Stay warm, it informed him, and burrowed into his parka again. Obviously, this was its way of travelling. He kind of got the feeling that it thought he was its mother. Skut bit his lip. Well, really there was no other choice open to him. He couldn't actually get back to Faraway Station. Not on his own. Not without a boat. And living out here... well, he could hunt. Trap fish. Find some kind of shelter. But he only had another mag of flechette charges. And he knew that mama and his father, when he got in, would be going absolutely spare. And, he thought guiltily, things were hard enough already. They didn't TELL him, but he knew. They were clinging on by their fingernails, and Highpoint Station was expensive. It was all about the high-end tourist trade—which meant that everything was expensive.

Besides, he was hungry. That was the problem, now, all the time. He was growing, which was why his trousers had split. They were too small. Even the parka was getting a bit short in the sleeves. At Faraway there had always been more food than they could eat. Here, it had to be bought, unless his father managed to bring fish home from the charter-boat.

Share meat It was plainly offering to let him enjoy some of the bloody piece of spill-deer belly. *Like fish* it informed him, squiggling itself into a more comfortable spot.

"And I am not allowed to keep you, either. They don't let native life-forms inside the barrier." Highpoint was fenced with a twenty-five foot concrete barrier-wall, and roofed in with a transparent plas-crete roof. It was one of the reasons that finding anywhere to stay was just so expensive. There wasn't much, outside of the hotels with their magnificent view of the bay, and the accommodation provided for staff and government employees. You weren't supposed to stay in Highpoint, except in a hotel. But with the situation like it was...all outstations had been instructed to come back there, while the war was on. And the way their charter was worded, as Papa explained, if they left Vann's World in less than twenty years, the title for Faraway Station reverted to the State.

A distant rumble made Skut aware of something he hadn't been expecting. It was an incoming ship! Maybe one full of tourists! That would bring more charters for his father to crew on, and even casual work for his mother, cleaning their rooms. PhD room-service, as she said. But it was probably just another lot of government bureaucrats, or some super-wealthy individual—they could still afford to travel.

Now, he just had to get back, safely. Vann's World above the tide line could be quite hard going, lots of little gullies and streams, but most of the native vegetation up here was quite low, grass-like, or thickets of willow-withy, mostly safe to walk though. There were stink-pod bushes, and the chance of a Loor, or a crocopede, and of course hamerkops and several other predatory fliers. They weren't really birds. He grinned to himself. The one way he could always get Mama to go off pop was to call them birds. She was a Xeno-Zoologist, and they were her field.

The ship had long landed by the time Skut got to the concrete wall that surrounded the settlement. He knew where he was heading for—exactly where he'd come out. The main gates had a guard, and detectors and sniffers to pick up contamination or native life. The laboratory, where they let Mama work, had its own door, and a little subsection containment lab for working on native species. The detectors on the inner door had broken some time back and no-one had fixed them. Back home, the station had a wall, but Papa's thinking was that they had to live with the local critters, and it would be better for them to learn how, so they did.

The only worry was that someone might be working in the containment lab, and worst of all, it would probably be his mother. The place had been pretty well let go since the war had started. Before that it had been used by visiting scientists and even a few post-grad students. Now it had cobwebs. Well, he didn't mind cobwebs, as long as he could get back unseen. But they might be looking for him by now. Maybe. He was supposed to be in school, and the headmistress liked sending nasty messages to his parents. He sighed. He was in trouble again. It was not like that was anything new. It seemed to Skut that he'd been in trouble since the day he arrived.

Skut put the flechette, holster, and his belt-knife into a little locker near the door. He'd have been in even more misery if they got confiscated, and they would be, if he wore them inside the station. The little creature in his shirt stirred and snuggled against him. He'd be in all sorts of trouble about that too. Oh well. What was one more thing to be in trouble about? He took a deep breath, squared his shoulders, and walked through the doorway into Highpoint. It was just like he left it, unfortunately. Neat, well-watered Earth plants, and paved walkways, under the plas-crete dome. He walked back down to the school, preparing his excuses. "You need to keep quiet and stay hidden inside my shirt," he informed it.

Quiet?

"Like we're being hunted and don't want to be seen or heard."

He had to go with hoping it understood, as he'd reached the school's playground gate. There were a few kids out there, playing around, mostly the younger ones. He took a deep breath, and headed for the classroom...which was empty.

Coming out onto the corridor again he snagged the second of two kids running past, letting, he realized, the one in front escape. "Where is everyone?"

The little boy struggled in his grip. "Let go of me. I'll tell teacher..."

"I'll let go of you. Just tell me what's happened to class."

"Ms. Bargen give all the kids off school if their parents said it was Okay."

Skut got it. It had been a while since there had been anything but a few luxury space yachts putting in. Goods had got a bit pricy and short. Things ordered from off-world hadn't arrived for several months. The Headmistress—and the teachers, most likely—had not wanted to wait until school closed and the two supermarkets in Highpoint had sold out of a lot of groceries again. "Crawf's still here. If you don't let go of me, I'll scream until he comes."

Crawf, or Mr Crawford, was the youngest teacher, and the only one Skut didn't detest. He actually knew a few things, unlike the rest of them. He let go of the kid, who bolted a bit down the corridor, then stopped and stuck his tongue out at Skut, then turned and ran again, yelling "Pru! I'll catch you. I'm going to sit on your head, you little worm!"

Skut put two and two together, and figured he'd saved the little girl, who had run past him first, a bit of torture, at least for now. Well! That was a bit of luck, school being closed. He might as well go to the apartment. He still wouldn't call it 'home.' That was, and always would be Faraway Station. He was hungry.

Hungry.

It wasn't urgent, just, well, fond of food.

That was going to be another problem, Skut foresaw.

TWO

Ted, or 'Podge' Greene, as he'd got kind of used to being called, not because he liked it, but because fighting it only made it stick harder—was enjoying the view of Vann's World from orbit. It was like a huge blue-and-white marble. He knew it was a water-world, shallow seas and endless chains of islands. They had orbited just inside the three massive moons while the ship got clearance to land. With the war that had been going on, that took time, these days.

"You'll like it, kids," his father had said, when they'd finally set out on the journey from Havilland to here. "It's not Metheglin, but, well, we can't go back there."

Podge hated that bit of pain in dad's voice whenever he mentioned Metheglin. They didn't talk about it much, because of that. His sister Maddy didn't even remember it that well—she'd only been six when they escaped. The last two years had been in a camp on Havilland. That had been something he'd happily forget. Yeah, the doctors had saved dad's life, if not his leg. The prosthesis worked well enough for it not to be obvious. But he just wanted to put all that behind them.

"Supposed to be the best fishing in all of human space," said his father, coming up behind the two of them, peering out of the massive forward view-screens. "I can't wait!"

Fishing...fishing was the reason they were still alive and here. They'd been out on a fishing trip when the Ghats had landed, and had destroyed half of the Honeyfall City, taking most of the people who had survived as prisoners, shipping them back to their home-worlds as slaves and hostages. Ted wasn't sure how he felt about going fishing. He wondered about the place they were coming to. He supposed it would be wild and exciting. He also wondered about the school he and Maddy were apparently going to. It would be different, after the huge classes in the Displaced Person's Camp. Here there were a hundred and seventy-eight kids, from littles to graduation, and he and his sister would bring that up to 180. At least it wouldn't be crowded.

The ship set down on the landing-field behind High-point Station. Ted soon discovered that all his ideas were basically wrong. For starters, it was cold. He'd never been to a tropical island, but he'd seen enough videos. Well, there weren't any palm trees, once they got inside the wall, just houses with grass and shrubs, all very tidy. Their new house was big and nice. It had a view down the edge of a hotel, through the plas-crete roof, across a corner of a blue-grey bay enclosed by two cliff-peninsulas. There was only one main road, which ran in a circle from the landing site and space-port, right around the settlement, basically, to the two huge hotels on the cliff sea-front and back to the spaceport. And... it was all roofed in. Which meant the place was really pretty small, and very built up. It wasn't as dense as the Displaced Person's Camp, but not far off.

"Why the roof?" he asked the woman who was showing them around. She was the 'General Manager,' and apparently the big cheese of the place. She thought so anyway. She fluttered her hands. "The wildlife is rather dangerous. Predatory birds, and nasty animals. So, it was decided that the government should be run from a protected place. Besides, the weather can be quite extreme."

The other thing he noticed was that the air was, besides cold, quite odd smelling. His mother commented. She would! That earned a disapproving sniff. "The scrubbers are supposed to clean it. It's one of the reasons Highpoint desperately needs a settlement engineer."

That was dad. His new job. His father didn't say anything, just smiled. That would have made Podge nervous. It didn't seem to work on the General Manager lady. She waffled on about the various jobs that had been waiting for someone to fill the position. Finally, dad said, "Sounds like a lot for one person. And you don't have a communications system. No 'phones?"

"Well, Carol—the settlement engineer before you—had a staff of seven, I think. But she struggled to keep them, and now with the war having crimped our tourist trade, we haven't the budget for that many. But you could employ a couple of farmers. The Confederated Planets Government ordered them all to come back here, after Metheglin. We can't protect them out there. They're desperate, and will work cheaply. Anyway, we talked about 'phones at Council, but really, the expense, and the place is small."

Fortunately, Maddy stepped in—or rather jumped in,

before their father lost the new job right then and there. "Why is this place so...so bouncy?" she demanded.

"Bouncy?" the woman repeated, puzzled. That was about normal with Maddy. Her brain worked in odd directions.

"Yes. Like this." She jumped. And touched the ceiling. Podge knew exactly what she meant. But he knew what it was.

"Ah," said mother, obviously trying not to laugh at the horrified face of the General Manager. "Lower gravity, dear. Havilland was 1.2 Earth, and Metheglin 1.1 G Earth-normal, and this 0.9G I think you said, Robert? So, we feel as if we're bouncing when we walk. Now, about the school," she said, changing the subject.

"Ah yes. The headmistress, Ms. Bargen, is excellent. They do have to share some classes as we don't have a lot of children here."

Podge just hoped he didn't end up in the same class as Maddy. "Podge," said his mother, "Wants to continue with advanced electronics. He was top of his class at the school on Havilland."

Podge felt his face go red. He wished mum wouldn't bring it up.

"Er...I...I don't know quite what technical subjects are available. It's not really my daughter Hillary's interest."

"We'll find out," said dad. "I can always teach him myself. In my ample spare time."

Being snarky plainly went over this woman's head. "We don't really permit home-schooling here at Highpoint. The farmers that came in, had mostly subjected their children to it. It made it very difficult to integrate them. Now, if you need to do any shopping, I would suggest Weltz-Herros rather than Loper's Supermarket. And I would say you'd be wise to get down today, quite soon. Supplies have been erratic, because of the war."

"Well, that should improve," said his father. "The Ghats have been knocked back on their heels, and so far, the cease-fire is holding."

"Just so. We've been in communication about some high-profile visitors, to try and get tourism going again. So, we will want the place looking its best soon, Mr Greene," she said waving a finger at him, and looking at him with half-lowered eyes.

"I will do my best," said dad calmly.

Well, he would. But he didn't sound terribly pleased. A lot of this was not what they'd been told, before. Now they were here...well, it was better than the DPP Camp on Havilland.

When she had gone, dad said as much. "Looks like we've been sold a bit of a pig in a poke, Mary. A thousand people—I thought it would leave me a bit of time for my own work. Now I hear it swells to nearly seven thousand when the hotels are full, and it is basically a sealed environment. And it doesn't sound like everything is too hunky-dory here. Just between us, that fellow I was talking to on the ship, yesterday. He's an auditor-investigator. Showed me his documentation, so I can't refuse to help him. He's arranged to come and visit my office tomorrow morning, before the ship leaves. Sounds like someone in government has been looking at the finances here." He grimaced. "At least it isn't me they can blame. I gather that's why he was willing to identify himself. Well, the pay is good, and a twelve-month stint should see us with enough money to move on."

That was before they went to the supermarkets, exploring both. They were close enough to walk, even with dad's prosthetic leg. He could walk pretty well on it, these days.

The prices were ridiculous at the first place, Weltz-Herros Emporium, that the GM had recommended. It was plainly very posh, and aimed at well-heeled tourists. It was noticeably cheaper at the second, but still twice the price of basic goods on Havilland. Dad said as much to the elderly man packing shelves.

The old man sighed. "Everything is imported. We used to get fish, vegetables, cereals, and some meat from the farms. But the farmers are not allowed to go back to their farms. Most gave up and went off-world if they could. The hotels do their own ordering, so business is not great. Believe me, I wouldn't be packing my own shelves if it was." He stuck out a hand. "I'm Wolfgang Loper, by the way. You'll be the new Town Engineer. You don't know anything about refrigeration systems, do you?"

"What's wrong?" his father asked.

"The computer keeps reading the temperature wrong, and switching the fridges off. I have to switch them on manually. I lost a fair bit of stock, because I didn't notice in time."

"That sounds like my boy's thing. Computers. I'm more of a hardware man," said his father. "Podge will have a look at it while we shop. The sight of all this food is making him hungry."

The old guy took Podge up to his office, introduced him to the woman working on order lists as his daughter Sarah, and left him to look at the computer set up to run the shop equipment. It was a quick fix—a minor programming glitch in the latest update to the system. He showed the lady and got told he was a marvel. She looked him up and down, smiled and said, "So, how old are you, young man?"

"Nearly twelve, Ma'am."

"It's a pity my Pru won't be in class with you then. She loves computers, but the teaching is pretty basic, I'm afraid. I have to go and fetch her from school. They let them off early because the ship came in. I just had to finish checking the order list first to see what we actually got. Let me take you down."

"I can set this up so it doesn't turn the fridge off, just sounds an alarm," said Podge. It was pretty basic, really.

"You can?" she said, looking pleased.

"Yeah, it's an option. Look. Here." He showed her on screen. "Just click 'alarm only.'"

"Do it! Pop will be so pleased. He's been getting up three times a night to check." Podge did so, and showed her how to undo it if she wanted to, then let her walk him back downstairs.

"You better keep this quiet," she said as they walked. "Or you'll be doing so much fixit, that you don't get any time for yourself. There's no-one really doing tech support here." She approached her father and tapped him on the arm. "Pop, listen, he's fixed it, and he's set an alarm for you if the fridges want to switch off, and they deserve a staff discount, and," she said, taking in Maddy, "A bag of Pru's favourite toffees."

Podge found that his parents were somewhat cheered—not only by saving money, but also by having talked to the shop owner. The situation now was much the worse because of the war, and maybe things would be coming back to normal soon. Besides, the toffees were indeed very good.

That wasn't something he was sure he thought of the school, though. Mum took them in to enrol them the next morning. He was put into a class with fifteen other kids in his grade. To his relief, Maddy was in the next class down. The kids all stared at him, curiously, when the Headmistress brought him in, but he had no chance to meet them. It was their grade, and the grade above, and he was handed some work to get on with—very basic maths. It took him a few minutes to do, and then, bored, he started designing a space-ship. He got rather absorbed in working out the fin-rake for atmospheric travel and aquatic landings, and didn't notice the teacher had stopped talking to the older kids and walked up behind him. She put a long-red nailed hand on his shoulder and dug her claws in, and said, icily, "What do you think you're doing?"

"Calculating stress vectors," he said, truthfully.

That was obviously not the right answer. She reached over and crumpled the beautiful design-drawing. Stuck her face right in his. "Don't get smart with me, young man. That's an hour's detention after school. Why haven't you done the mathematics exercises? Too hard for you? We'll have to put you down a class or two."

"I have," protested Ted. "Here. See." He pointed to the completed workbook. She snatched it up. Looked at it as if she might destroy that too, then made a noise like a pig with a stomach ache. "You copied this!"

"No, I didn't," he protested. "It's easy stuff."

"Give me your workbook, Linda," snapped the teacher, to the girl next along the row of desks.

"I haven't finished, Miss," said the girl, alarmed.

"Give it to me anyway. I will see what he copied."

She peered at both workbooks. "Hmph." Obviously, whatever she was looking for, she didn't find. "Well. I can tell you're going to be a problem. You can move to the front next to Harkkson, so I can keep my eye on you."

So, Podge found himself moved to the front row, into a vacant seat next to a tall, skinny boy with hair so blond it was almost white. The boy gave him a quick look of wary sympathy, before the teacher spoke again.

"Right, five minutes to recess. Grade 7's, finish up those exercises, and Grade 8, complete those essays. I want them on my desk in two neat piles." She slapped Podge's workbook in front of him. "Redo that. It's untidy."

THREE

Skut had been grateful to the ship for at least getting him out of trouble. He soon realized that looking after the little animal was going to be even harder that he'd guessed. If it wasn't asleep it was permanently two things: hungry and curious. If it hadn't felt so...dependent, and...and, well, trusting, he wouldn't be doing such a crazy thing. The apartment they rented was really only one room, and not a big one at that. He had a little area in the back corner, separated off by a couple of cupboards, which had room for a mattress, and lines strung above it for his clothes. There hadn't been time to pack up much else on Faraway, before being crammed into the jet-boat with five other frightened farmer families. There hadn't been space either. They hadn't really known what was going on.

Thinking back, he realized that of the families on the boat, they were only ones that were still sitting at Highpoint. The others had given up and left. There was a note from mama on the table. 'Got a bit of work at the hotel, unloading. Supper for you and Papa in the crock-pot. Love you.'

That was a relief. He didn't have to worry about the creature being seen. He opened his parka and it popped out, looking quizzically around. *Safe?*

"Safe as houses."

Houses?

Skut understood this as a word. Some of what the creature was sort of 'saying' was more like a concept he translated, things they both understood. This, along with 'excuse me' were things that it seemed to have no idea what it actually meant. Well, there had been no sign of civilization on Vann's world or they would never have been allowed to land, let alone have colonists. These little things probably didn't build houses. What would they build with?

Looking at it carefully, it did have a sort of three-clawed hand on its forelegs, and the back ones...were flippers, with nails. Vann's World's animals had a six—or more, legged pattern. He'd seen it fly briefly...so...wings? On cue it unfolded those out, little wings with lots of trailing filaments, and leapt into a brief flight to the cupboard top. Then it flew erratically around the room. He could see that it was built to fly, it just wasn't much good at it yet. He was worried it might crash into something, but it managed a circuit without doing more than knocking the wall-clock askew. Before it launched into flight again and did destroy something, Skut thought he'd better distract it.

"Hey, can you play catch?"

Catch with a grabbing fish image came into his mind.

"Yeah. But you don't eat it. It is just for practice, see."

He had a couple of ping-pong balls, and he sat on his bed, and tossed one up in air. "Catch!"

It took a few tries for the little creature to get the hang of it, and it bit a hole in one of the balls and *tastes horrible* he was informed.

"Don't bite it. Just catch it."

For half an hour they had the most fun Skut had had since he came to Highpoint. The animal grew rapidly better at the game and they moved past him tossing the ball directly to it, to him trying to get the ball past it, and then the creature dive-bombing him with the ball and releasing it like a torpedo. It was fast and very agile, and plainly getting used to using its wings, more and more. And then suddenly it said *tired* and dived into the front of his shirt, still clutching the wounded ping-pong ball.

It was just in time, as it happened. His father came in, hands dirty from the little patch of garden outside the back of the poky room. He'd obviously stopped there on his way in from work. Papa could no more stop farming than he could stop breathing, and the vegetables saved them from going hungry. "Hey, Skutter! I heard you laughing inside, so I left you to it."

"Ah. Just playing a silly game, Papa."

"Well, it did my heart good to hear you laugh. I thought you must have a friend. Mama has gone to help unpack, yes? The skipper let us go early because he wanted to get to the shop. Maybe it brings us some customers." Pay for being at sea was a bit higher, so that would be good news. "Now, what do we have for food?"

Food. It was sleepy comment.

"Later," said Skut, hastily.

"Oh no," said his father. "We eat now. Mama would not want the food to spoil, then I can get another hour in before the light is all gone."

"Uh. Sure. I'll come and help you. I just have some...stuff I have to do."

"No problem, my son. Homework on a day like today," said his father dishing up for them. "I thought you had a friend in here. Doing homework was always my excuse to go to Knut's house," he said, smiling. It was always good to see Papa smile, it made the worry lines go away for a bit. "But it looks like you have no-one you get on with, since Billy Osmond's family moved off-world. Well, maybe things will turn around."

It hadn't been too bad, at first, in the school. There'd been a bunch of new kids, all from the outlying farms. They could stick together. But there were no more in his grade or class, as families had given up and left. Skut ate slowly, to the extent that father asked if he was feeling all right?

"Oh fine, Papa. I was just thinking about something we did at school. You go on. I will wash the plates and come join you."

"You want to tell me about it?"

"No. It's...it's not important."

"I can still listen. Anytime."

"Thank you, Papa. But it's not something you can do anything about. I just wish we could go home again."

His father sighed. "Ja. It has been a long eighteen months, but surely, now they have a ceasefire...but the problem is, those Ghats...they have no honor, son. To lie and cheat someone who is not a Ghat, is fine for them. They broke the last ceasefire, and the one before. It could be two years, it could be twenty. Meanwhile we sit here."

Skut nodded, but the longing for home was like a knife in his stomach. The little creature stirred and snuggled against him. Somehow that helped a bit.

His father went out to go on working in his little garden, and Skut opened his shirt a bit. "I've left you some food. And if you don't hurry up and eat it, I'm starving myself." Skut had kept back the meat in the stew, and the fluffy creature sniffed at it, and then began to eat like he hadn't had a Hamerkop drumstick and a strip of spill-deer already that afternoon. *excuse me!* it informed him with something like glee.

It didn't want the potato or the greens, and Skut was glad to eat those himself. He was still hungry even if the little furry animal wasn't. They didn't have meat every night. It was too expensive. How was he going to feed it? "Now," he said, pushing that aside. "You stay quiet in my shirt. I must go out and help Papa," he informed it.

Sleepy.

"Good. You mustn't get seen, okay?"

It cooperated, as he went to help tend the rows of peas, carrots, and hills of potatoes. The tiny patch was just two raised beds, and a little potato patch—absolutely jammed with food plants. The soil of Vann's World was volcanic and fertile, just like its seas.

That night, other than a midnight snuffle around under his blankets for a missing ping-pong ball, passed peacefully. Oh, and when he took it to the bathroom, and it tried to drink from the toilet bowl, he gave it water in the hand-basin, and explained what the toilet was for. To his surprise it understood, and used it. Well, that was one problem solved! But long before dawn, it was up, and saying *hungry.*

Dressing quietly, Skut took a torch, slipped out of the apartment past his sleeping parents, walked up to the Containment Lab door, and out. It was all he could think of to do. There wasn't spare food...and it seemed to be a meat-eater. Muesli and milk likely wouldn't do. He strapped on his belt-knife and flechette, and slipped out of the door in the concrete wall, glad the lock was still unfixed.

The last of Vann's World's three moons was sinking. The Spill-deer's little cousin, the Patratti, were using Highpoint's wall as a convenient shelter, and were as surprised to see him as he was them. He missed his first shot because of that, but not the second. He wasn't that experienced at gutting but he managed it, despite a little furry pest trying to take bites while he was working. "Stop it. I'm trying to make sure you have food."

Hungry!

He cut it a strip of meat to keep it quiet. The Patratti, gutted, still weighed about six or seven pounds. He carried it back carefully so he didn't get blood on himself, and was glad it was so close to the door.

There was an unused fridge inside the containment lab, that mother had sometimes used to keep extra fish in when Papa had managed to bring some back from a charter. He had to cut the patratti in half to get it in, but his little pest was happy and quiet, and he had food for it for a while. He wouldn't have said 'no' to a patratti leg himself—they used to eat it often at Faraway, but he had no way of cooking it. And he really didn't want Mama and Papa in on this. They had enough trouble. He took another strip of meat, put it into a sample-bag and put that in his pocket for later.

Then he put away the knife and flechette pistol, and hurried back home. His parents were awake and up now, so he got in before the question. "I went for a walk. It's better when no-one is around."

"Ja." Papa nodded. "It feels like there is more space."

All things considered, Skut thought he'd brushed through pretty well. He wasn't looking forward to school, but the little creature was fed, and contentedly snuggled inside his shirt with the ping-pong ball.

FOUR

S kut timed it very carefully, getting into the school grounds exactly one minute before the bell for class to start. Ms. Sanders droned some bad explanation of square roots—stuff he'd covered in home-schooling two years back. She handed out workbooks. He was used to working on a computer, and his handwriting wasn't good—but that was the only thing that stopped him finishing in five minutes. And then there was an interruption. The headmistress brought a new kid to the class. First look wasn't inspiring. He was short and fat with lank curly dark hair. He had a round face too, that didn't show much expression. Bland and blank.

Then the new kid got carrots from the Vulture with her red claws, and got punished by being sent to sit next to Skut. That was the Vulture's way of getting her pets to make the kid's life a misery. Well, it might take them off making his life a misery. He felt rather sorry for the kid.

As they walked out into the small grassed area for recess, the new kid just plainly following the crowd, the first of the pets, that creep Warren, who liked to beat up littler kids, grabbed the new boy by both lapels of his jacket. "Listen, fatty. You stay back and let the seniors pass. Where are you from, anyway?"

Already the mean girls club were forming a circle, and giggling in anticipation.

The fat kid moved fast. He grabbed Warren by the front of his coat...and picked him up off the floor. "Metheglin. It's a high gravity world, pudding-brain," he said, shaking Warren like a crocopede does its prey. "I'm stronger than you. Don't pick on me, or I'll sit on you. They call me Podge because being sat on me will leave you squashed." And he threw Warren back among the mean girls, where he landed on his butt with a crash and a whoof of breath.

Skut couldn't help smiling. Warren had made his life hell for a few months after Billy left. He hadn't lately, because although he still weighed a lot more than Skut, Skut was now four inches taller than he was. He saw that the new kid was about to walk off, and he knew Warren. "Hey. New kid, Podge," he said, warningly. "Don't turn your back on him."

"Ooh, you've got new friend," said Jaccie. She was, of the three mean girls in the grade above, the most spiteful. They all sucked up to Hillary, and when Hillary was nasty, she was very nasty, but Jaccie was always the one looking to show off to her crowd. She was a big girl, not very bright, and followed Hillary's lead and did her enforcing. She was fond of hitting and scratching, especially those that couldn't fight back. "No one told you he wears pink underwear...Podge?" she said disdainfully. Like she had room to call someone 'Podge.'

Skut felt his face go red. The new kid, however, laughed. "No, but they said there was a fat, ugly girl who doesn't wear any pants at all, in the grade above me. That would be you, right?"

Jaccie stood frozen with outrage. Worse, for her, was that Skut and some of the other kids were laughing. "Not me! How dare you say that! I'll...I'll..."

"Well," said Podge. "You could show us. I mean I can see the fat and ugly part, so..."

She rushed at him screaming, claws out to scratch. Skut caught her arm. "You'll get into trouble if you fight," he said.

Her reaction to that was to try and scratch him with the other hand. The new kid caught that. She tried to bite and kick, in between screams, which inevitably attracted one of the teachers from down the corridor.

"What is going on here?" demanded the Vulture, like she hadn't encouraged it.

"They're being mean to me, Miss," whined Jaccie.

"Those boys were very rude," said Hillary.

"And," said Warren, "Hitting a girl. That's not allowed," he said, like he didn't do it all the time.

"I haven't hit anyone," said Podge. "And neither has this guy," pointing a thumb at Skut. "Just tried to stop her scratching us."

Skut realized it might have been better if he'd let Jaccie get a scratch in. But, worryingly, the little creature in his shirt had moved up his sleeve. *Bite?* *Zap?*

"No," said Skut, hoping that answered for both his pet and the Vulture. "They were being mean to the new kid, Miz."

The Vulture sniffed. "You need to treat the girls and

seniors with respect. Harkkson, new boy…Greene, you can both have an hour's detention. You're not off to a good start are you, Greene? I've got you under my eye from now on. Now run along, all of you. I need my tea."

"Take you to a safe-ish spot," Skut offered, as they moved off.

"Thanks. Phew, I thought school in the DPP was rough. That teacher's a cow, isn't she?"

"I like cows," said Skut. "I call her the Vulture, with those claws and the way she hangs over you."

Podge grinned, which made his expressionless face something else entirely. "Good name. Sorry you got detention too."

Skut shrugged. "It's not that bad, Crawf takes it, and he's all right." He smiled wryly. "I'm used to it. I spend some time there. There's not a lot else to do."

"Can't we go exploring, or go to the beach, or go fishing?" said Podge. Skut cast him a wary glance…and he saw Podge's eyes narrow slightly. "You can trust me. I won't split."

"We're not allowed to," was all Skut was prepared to venture. "I'm from one of the farms. I'm not used to being locked up. But they say it is too dangerous out there."

"And is it?" asked Podge, curiously.

"Sort of," Skut admitted. "If you don't know what you're doing. But my father started training me from when I was little. He said they couldn't watch me all the time, and I had to be able to look after myself."

"What's it like out there?"

"Like being alive. This place is like being in jail," he said, bitterly. "And school is the worst. Mama taught me, and it's all so basic here."

"Yeah. That math was kiddie stuff," agreed the new kid. "Say, what's your name?"

"Skut."

"Scoot?"

"Yes, sort of." No one would ever pronounce it right, and he wasn't going to tell anyone his full name. They'd tease him, more.

The kid stuck out his hand. "My name is actually Ted. But I get called Podge...and if you show them it upsets you, they tease you."

Skut shook his hand, aware that the little creature was up his sleeve, threatening to stick its head out. "The mean girls club are going to do that anyway, and the Vulture and old Bargen-basement do nothing to stop them," he said sourly.

Podge laughed. "Bargen-basement! I didn't like her much either."

At this point they were interrupted by two little girls, the one with red hair, literally bouncing up and down, and the other—a small dark girl, looking shy and moderately terrified. "This is my big brother Podge," announced the bouncer. "This is my new best friend, Pru. I said you would splatter the brains of that nasty boy if he touched her again. And all his friends. I hit two of them."

"Oh Maddy," said Podge, and sighed. "I'm not your army, you know."

"Yes, you are," she informed him, grinning from ear to ear. "Who is your friend?"

"I'm Skut," he said, unable to resist the kid's grin.

Little Pru, who was clinging to her bouncing friend, said something quietly to her. "Ah. You're the one that helped her get away from that Tim Herros yesterday. I like you. Now I have two armies!"

"And two leggies," said her brother. "Use them to run off somewhere else. Skut and I are talking."

"Let them stay close," Skut found himself saying. "That Herros kid is Warren's younger brother, and he's a terror too, bullying the little ones."

Podge sighed. "She never stops talking, Skut."

"I do," the red-head informed him, loudly.

"There you go again."

Hungry

Podge, who was also sitting on the bench, said: "Do they feed us?"

"Next recess," said Skut, standing up. "I got to go to the bathroom before the bell. We have Crawf for the next class. He's okay."

He took the little creature into the bathroom. Gave it some meat, and wondered how long he could keep this up for. Anyway, that new boy seemed okay.

PODGE WRINKLED HIS BROW, and looked at his sister, who was busy drawing something in the dirt with her boot—some game she planned to teach her new friend. "Did either of you hear Skut say he was hungry?"

"No. Now look, Pru, you jump over the line here. And then there you hop..."

"Did either of you say so?"

"No, it's only you that is hungry all the time, big brother.

I liked him. No, Pru, you've got to hop on your left foot, then skip."

The bell to signal the end of recess rang and Podge joined the other kids barging into the corridor, saw Skut just ahead of him, and followed. It helped that Skut was tall and had white-blond straight hair. It made him easy to follow. The next class, Geography, was actually relatively interesting. The only part that was a bit awkward was that the teacher made him stand up and introduce himself. "Greene, is it? And what do we call you?"

"Uh. Podge, Sir."

"Well, Podge, so where are you from? If I ask you the questions here it'll save you having to answer it over and over.

"Um, Metheglin, Sir. And then eighteen months in the DPP camp on Havilland."

"I see. You were one of the hostages?" There was sympathy in his voice.

"No, Sir. They only got them back about five months ago. We didn't get captured. We weren't in Honeyfall City, when the Ghat ships landed. We hid out with the guerrillas. My...my parents were fighting the Ghats." He did not go on with something that was already making him feel angry again. They had beaten the Ghats, fought them to a standstill, until they fled with their prisoners. And then the Government had given Metheglin to them anyway, in exchange for the hostages and a cease-fire.

"I see," said the teacher again, slowly. "You've seen things few of us can imagine. If you need to talk about it, my door is always open. Still, you'll enjoy the peace and security of Vann's World. We have an excellent defensive missile system, which would make an offensive landing anywhere with a few hundred miles impossible. Class, I think we all need to welcome young Podge, and please be kind to him. It's hard coming to a new place."

Podge nodded, swallowed and sat down, hastily. Honestly, it was easier to cope with nasty than nice. But somehow, he did feel like someone said *Safe. Warm*

The class finished, and they went in a mob to the cafeteria. The lunch was not up to his mother's standards, but it was OK. He'd eaten worse, and he was perpetually hungry at the moment. He sat with Skut. They were alone at the table, until his sister and her new little follower came to sit with them. The little follower, her eyes wide whispered urgently to her. "I don't care," Maddy said loudly. "He's my brother, I want to sit with him and Skut. I don't want to sit with the little kids. They're all smelly. Anyway, who makes us not sit with them?"

"The seniors say we can't," said Pru, timidly.

"Sit down girls," said Mr Crawford, walking along the aisle between the tables. He was plainly on cafeteria duty. "Nice to see a family together."

"Tell 'em Crawf said you had to," advised Skut, to the plainly terrorized Pru.

"They will catch us after school," she said in a terrified whisper.

"Is your mamma coming to fetch you?" asked Skut.

Pru nodded.

"You stick in the classroom when the bell rings," said Skut. "Podge and me will walk you out. The mean girls know we both have detention, so they won't be hanging about for us."

They got a tremulous smile of thanks. Little Pru did relax and eat her food under his sister's cheerful pushing, Podge noticed. She even laughed a few times and started not whispering. He wondered if Maddy knew how much she sounded like mum. She was playing that, sort of.

Skut asked him about what the worlds he'd come from were like.

"The camp sucked. I...I really loved Metheglin. We went fishing a lot. It's my dad's favorite thing."

"Mine too," Maddy informed them. "Podge would rather play with his computer."

"I used to fish a lot at home," said Skut. "Papa...my father said we don't go fishing here, we go catching. He says on his old home, you could fish all day and maybe catch an old boot."

"I never catch anything," said Podge. "It might be more interesting if I did. So, what sort of fish do you get here?" Anything to lead conversation away from memories of Metheglin.

Skut told him—at length, and kept them entertained until the bell rang. Podge was beginning to decide he liked Skut. His clothes were a little old and tight, but that was one thing that they'd all been through in the DPP camp. He seemed to understand that Podge didn't want to talk, and made up for it. He wasn't boasting, just very matter of fact about fishing in all sorts of ways, and talking about the different targets. He obviously knew and loved it and, it seemed, missed it. Every second sentence seemed to be a mention of this place he came from—Faraway Station—a name, once the explanation was demanded by Maddy, she thought the best of jokes. He was going to get sick of that, he could tell.

The one weird thing Podge struggled to get his head around, was he was sure he'd seen Skut slip a piece of meat into his sleeve. That seemed a bit yuck. Maybe they didn't have food at home? He was skinny enough for that to be true. Maybe he hadn't actually done that...

They kept their word to the girls, and arrived to a scene of battle. Maddy was swinging her school-bag around like a club, trying to push through to the door. Little Pru had just been knocked over by one of the boys. Plainly, the two had stayed behind—and their tormentors had come back for them.

"My brother has come to splatter your brains," said Maddy with great relish. That, he was glad, didn't prove necessary, as they all fled.

They walked along to the gate. The Junior kids were only allowed to leave if a parent came to fetch them, and Podge's mother was waiting, but there was no sign of a parent for Pru. Podge's mother accepted with a wry smile his telling her that he and Skut had detention to go to, and would be home later. "You can't stay out of trouble for long, can you?" she said with a sigh.

"It follows me around, Mum," he replied with a shrug.

"Mum," Maddy informed her mother, "This is my friend Pru. We have to stay here until her mummy comes."

FIVE

Podge and Skut walked back to the classroom, to await their punishment. "It's just boring," said Skut. "It's usually Crawf. They give him all the extra duties."

So it proved. Mr Crawford came in, looked at the two of them, and said, raising his eyebrows: "Running afoul of Ms. Sanders already. Well, I will have to throw you into the briar patch. How is your math, Greene?"

"Uh. Pretty fair, Sir."

"And Harkkson can't even add," he said. "Well, I shall have to set you several maths exercises that will take you at least an hour to complete," he said, handing a worksheet to them. "Ms. Sanders will think that the cruellest I could be. When you're done you can turn them in to me. I shall go and make myself a cup of coffee and have a sandwich. Behave yourselves."

When he'd gone, and closed the door behind him, Podge said to Skut: "Do you really struggle with math? I can help. This is stuff I did last year."

Skut grinned. "The year before for me. My Mama taught me. He's joking. He doesn't like the Vulture either. He taught me math last year, so he knows. She gets stuff wrong, and doesn't understand it. But we better get busy, because the Vulture has sometimes stopped in on her way home to check that the kids are doing detention."

Sure enough, she did. "What are you doing?" she demanded.

"Maths," said Podge. "It's frightfully hard, Miz. It will take me hours and hours."

She smiled thinly. "See you finish it. And learn a lesson, both of you."

She left. Skut held his finger to his lips just as Podge was about to pack up, laughing. He pointed at the door, and tapped his ear.

They waited. And then Skut nodded. "She's gone. She caught Billy and me like that, once."

"She's something else!"

"Yeah. She doesn't like boys, and...and me, most of all."

"I beat you," said Podge, grinning. "I got two hours, you only got one."

"Lucky it's Crawf. He won't make us stay. Oh, yeah, a tip, make one small mistake. It makes her happy, otherwise she takes marks off untidiness. Her pets have to get top marks, which means we have to be marked down. How far have you got?"

"Another two questions."

"And I have one more. If we get it done before he gets back, Crawf will likely let us go.

They bent to it. It really wasn't hard stuff.

SKUT HAD RACED through the worksheet. It was not hard, but that was not the reason. The reason was that the little creature in his shirt was definitely getting restless. *Hungry* wasn't urgent, yet, as it had been before.

"Boy, I am starving!" said Podge. "Suddenly started thinking 'hungry.'"

Starving it was almost tasting the word.

"Yeah," said Podge. "Did you say that?"

"Uh. Yes," said Skut.

"Good thing mum packed me lunch then. I didn't know if we got school lunch. Fancy something?"

Starving!

"Oh, shut up!" Skut said. "Oh. Uh...not you Podge. Just...just something. I...I can't tell you," he said awkwardly falling over his tongue. "It's a secret."

"That's OK," said Podge, plainly puzzled. "Do you mind if I eat?"

"No. No. Just don't get caught. We're not allowed to eat in the classrooms."

Starving!

PODGE HAD BEEN LOOKING at Skut. opening his lunch-box. He'd heard that. But Skut's lips hadn't moved.

Skut grunted with irritation. "Don't." Then he looked at Podge. "Please, please don't tell anyone. They'll kill it. I am not allowed to have it. But it's only a baby, and it'll die if I don't look after it."

And suddenly a little electric-blue head popped out of Skut's collar, and stared at him with dark eyes, and a flaring of the mane around its small face.

"Wow! What is it?" asked Podge, staring open-mouthed.

Skut shrugged. "I dunno. I found it on the lowest tide-flat. It was scared, hungry, and cold. So...so I kept it."

The creature squirmed out of Skut's shirt, moving with an almost liquid grace. *Hungry. Starving*

"It's...it's talking inside my head," said Podge, feeling his eyes go wide.

"Yeah, it hasn't got a lot of words. Look, you haven't got a bit of meat or fish to spare, have you? That's what it eats. It's a little pig. I don't how I am going to keep it fed and not get caught."

"I'll help you! Help you hide it. Help you feed it."

He could see the doubt on Skut's face. And somehow, he told him, what he had told no-one else for the last two years. "I must. I have to. See, they killed my dog. They caught us, and the Ghats killed my dog while I had to watch." He could feel the tears he'd kept bottled up for years suddenly start to run down his cheeks.

"Oh...I...I am sorry," said Skut awkwardly.

Podge found the little furry thing was nuzzling against his cheek. *Warm.*

It was startling enough to make him stop crying. "Warm?"

"Like I said, it doesn't have a lot of words. I think it is trying to...to say it's OK," said Skut. "When it was scared and miserable, after the hamerkops had been at it, that's what it wanted."

"Oh. Well Warm to you too, little one. I'm sorry I started to blub."

"I would too," said Skut. "That's horrible. What...what happened?"

"We got rescued later that day. The Ghats walked into an ambush some of the farmers had set up. They got killed instead."

"Good!" said Skut.

Podge nodded. And the little blue streak of fur informed them *Hungry.*

Podge knew his laughter was a bit weak, but it helped. He opened his lunch-box. "Sausage?" he said, holding it out.

It didn't wait, just snatched it and flew back to Skut's desk.

"Greedy pig," said Skut, also laughing. And then "shush!" He shoved the furry little animal—and the sausage, into his shirt. Podge had the brains to tuck away his lunch-box, and they were both heads down and apparently hard at work when the door opened. Whoever it was didn't stay, just closed the door again. But Podge, wise now to the fact that Skut knew what went on, waited until Skut said, "Phew. That was close. Bargen."

"How did you know she was coming?

"I could hear her walking down the stairs to the corridor. One of the slats is loose, and makes a kind of slappy noise."

Scuse me.

Skut smiled. "That's what it says when it's full and satisfied. Because it burped and I said it should say that."

Podge grinned. "So, what is it, exactly?"

Skut shrugged. "I don't know. I've never seen one before, or even heard of one. We don't really know much about the animals on Vann's World. I mean, most of it is ocean. Especially the tropical zone. The storms are pretty wild up there. I found it on the lowest tide-tier, so it might even be that it normally lives in the sea."

"But it can fly."

"It's not good at it yet, but yes."

"What's its name? I mean, what do you call it?"

"I hadn't really thought of a name. Its...its just been with me."

"Well, you could ask it," said Podge.

Skut put his hand in his shirt and pulled it out. It was like a sinuous ribbon of bright blue fur. With little clawed feet, and a sharp snout and two forward looking dark eyes. It was holding something bright orange in its claws. "Ping-pong ball," explained Skut. "Hey little one, what's your name."

Name? He could read its puzzlement. It was...it was *itself.* It knew itself. It wasn't quite like any of others. It was *Itself.*

"I guess when you read minds, a name isn't important," said Podge. "But Skut and me don't. You know that we're different. His name is Skut and mine is Podge. Well, everyone calls me that."

Name same self?

That was a puzzler. "I think it means is a name the same as what it is," said Podge. "And I suppose...I dunno. Kind of."

"It's how we call each other," explained Skut. "We can't talk in each other's heads. You want me, you call 'Skut'. Then I know you mean me, not Podge."

They could almost feel the puzzlement as the little animal tried to work this out. *Skut.* *Podge.*

"Yeah. Are you being snarky?"

Snarky

It was a pronouncement. *Skut.* *Podge.* *Snarky.* *SNARKY!*

"I guess it has a name," said Skut with a wry smile. "Hush, I hear someone."

The someone proved to be Mr. Crawford. "And how are you going with the exercises?"

Podge wondered if he should claim to still be busy, but Skut said: "Done, Sir." So, he said the same.

"Well," said the school-master, a smile twitching under his bushy moustache. "I am sure that feels like an hour to you. And Greene, I'll give you an hour's credit as a welcome to the school."

"Uh. Thank you, Sir."

"Right, get out of here, both of you, I have marking to do, and the headmistress is gone."

So, they went. "What do you do after school here?" asked Podge as they walked out the gate.

Skut shrugged. "Go home. Lot of the kids head for the central park. Trouble is, it's the same kind of thing as at school, except there's no teachers around. But the special ones have passes to the hotel recreation rooms, so that takes the mean girls and their friends out of a lot of it. Um. I have to get some more food for Snarky."

Food! Snarky food!

"We'd better get him some."

Skut looked warily at him. "I've got some hidden in a fridge in bio-control. But my mother might be there. It's...it's supposed to be locked, only there's an emergency door that isn't."

"Cool. Let's go. My mum won't expect me for a bit. I told

her we have detention."

"We'll get into more serious trouble if we get caught. But mother said there was some kind of meeting this afternoon, that she and Papa were going to."

They walked through the small town that backed onto the massive hotels between them and the sea. It was all pretty ordinary. No real trees, but lots of shrubs and lawns, a couple of apartment blocks.

Skut led him along to a hedge of tall bushes, looked around, and then slipped between them. Podge followed. "The gate's a bit further on, but there's a house across the road from it," explained Skut. There was a small lawn area, slightly un-mowed, and a low huddle of buildings against the concrete fence. Like the lawn, it looked like it had been a while since anyone had bothered to paint it. "There's another gate next to the landing field, but Billy and I got caught going out of that one. It was just bad luck, 'cause there's no one around up there most of the time. They've locked it now." They walked across to the door, and Skut paused and listened carefully at it, before opening it, and listening again. He gave a thumbs-up and they slipped in.

It was obvious to Podge that Skut found the place ordinary, but it was pretty weird to him. There were shelves and shelves of dead plants, and lot of empty cages. There were also a few full shelves with strange plants in their containers, with water flooding them. Some were in glass-faced tanks. "Tide simulation," explained Skut when he asked. "Like we have the three tides." He pointed to some cages with little fluttering creatures in them. "Those are my mother's birdies." He grinned. It was kind of unusual as Skut looked very serious most of the time. "Don't call them that to her face, though. She says they just look like birds."

Tasty

"Don't you dare eat them, Snarky!" said Skut. "I've got you some Patratti."

Want birdies

"They're my mother's. You can't have them."

He got a piece of bloody meat out of the little fridge, and the blue Snarky scrambled out of his shirt front and grabbed it in its front claws, and started chewing away. *Still want birdies.*

"I guess that's the one thing that's worse about Snarky than my sister. Snarky can talk with his mouth full. What did you say you were feeding him?"

"Patratti. Sort of like very small deer."

"Where do you get them?"

Skut looked faintly guilty. "Outside. But we're not supposed to go there."

"Yeah. Another thing we're not supposed to do. If it is interesting or fun, you can't do it," said Podge, irritated.

"Yes," said Skut, a little doubtfully. "But it is sort of dangerous out there, Podge."

"You go out there."

"Yes, but my father taught me a lot of stuff. And I can shoot..."

"So can I."

"You can?"

"We were on Metheglin when the Ghats came. We got taught," said Podge, a bit terse about it.

"I didn't think of that...well, don't tell them at school. There was a big fuss about the farm kids bringing their weapons to school. Bargen-basement had a fit. But...I mean Podge, you wouldn't know what a stinger or a Hamerkop looked like, or what they do."

"I could learn. You could show me. It would be more fun than sitting around in here."

Skut still didn't look convinced, but Snarky having finished the piece of meat, chose that moment to go and fly over and pester the birdy things, he had other problems. He grabbed at the little creature, which seemed to think by the *fun* that it was a great game. Then Skut suddenly looked around in alarm and put his finger to his lips and beckoned. Podge noticed that Snarky hurtled back to the shelter of Skut's shirt, as the two them ducked behind a big rack of plants, just before the door opened.

"I suppose it is better we talk here, Helga, than upset the boy," said a deep male voice, with just a hint of a foreign accent. "But we can't go on like this. With the cease-fire they should let us go home! It's not right!"

"Yes, but it didn't help you shouting at them," answered a crisp female voice. "Or me. I cannot leave anyway with the baby due so soon."

There was a sigh. "I am sorry, Helga. I was so sure..."

"It will come, Nils. It will come."

"Yes, but we cannot afford the rent here forever."

"Maybe there will be more tourists. I can pick up work then. And you should get more charter trips," said the woman.

"I'll have to. We've nearly finished the last servicing and repainting work. What has upset your birdies?"

"They are not birdies, Nils," she said, sternly.

"Ja. But something has upset them."

"Well, let me feed them now that you are here to help me. Come and carry for me."

"For you, of course," he said.

As the footsteps faded, Skut grabbed Podge's arm and hustled him to the door, and then very nearly dragged him across to the shrubbery. "Phew. That was close," he said once they were there.

"Who was that?" asked Podge, although he had a pretty good idea.

"My parents," said Skut, glumly. "The government obviously won't let us go back to the farm."

"Thing is," said Podge, "Everyone expects the Ghats to break the ceasefire. They have every time, my father says. As soon as they are losing, they ask for a ceasefire."

"They shouldn't ever give them one," said Skut.

Podge gave a snort. "Now you sound like my father. But they always take hostages, and they'll kill them unless they get what they want."

"We should take hostages too then."

"Except they don't care. So, where do we go now?"

Want chase Snarky informed them.

"Chase?"

"He likes to chase a ping-pong ball." Skut hesitated. "We could go up to the back edge of the landing field. No one goes up there. I would take him home, but my father obviously isn't working, and...and it's pretty small. Only one room really. Got a cupboard dividing off a piece for me."

"Well, there is my place, but Maddy would drive you nuts. Let's go to the landing field."

It was a large area—walled but not roofed, up and behind the little town. You could see the bay from up here, with jetties protruding out from the hotels. "Do you go fishing down there?" Podge asked, after catching his breath.

"Guess what. We're not allowed onto the jetties. Paying guests only," said Skut, sourly. "It's the only place you could get into deepish water in the enclosed area. There are the slipways for the charter-boats a level down, but you can't get in there without a secure pass-key. Like an electronic thing."

"Oh. I know how to program those," said Podge. "We had them at the DPP camp."

"Yeah. Well, these ones don't work half the time. I sneaked down a couple of times and fished off the lower jetty —they're under the high jetty, and just there for the first and second tide. But they fixed them. Here Snarky. Let's have the ball."

They spent the next half an hour playing a complicated game of chase and catch with the little blue flying streak of fur. That led to a shocking surprise. As Podge was about to snatch the ball out of the air before Snarky could get to it...a spark leaped from the creature's streaming wing-tendrils.

"Yowch!" yelped Podge, wringing his hand. "You shocked me, you little brute."

Instantly, Snarky fluttered to his shoulder *Warm?*

It was plainly apologetic. Podge on the other hand was just incredulous. "It shocked me, Skut. Like, quite a wallop."

"Yeah. It seems to be able to do that. I don't think it meant to. Did you Snarky?"

Regret.

It was kind of hard to be mad at something that you can feel is sorry, and is butting its furry face against your chin. "It's OK. Just don't do that again. You packed a powerful amount of voltage."

Bigger. More.

"I think it's saying that when it's bigger it'll be even more able to shock," said Skut. "I think Snarky is still pretty much a baby."

"Then you really don't want a shock from a full size one. How big do they get?"

"I dunno, never seen anything quite like him before. How big do you get, Snarky? How big are your mum and dad?"

You and then *mum* *cold* *scared.* It dived into Skut's shirt and burrowed itself away.

"It's Ok, Snarky. We'll look after you. Me and Podge will look after you. Right, Podge?"

"Sure. But please don't shock me again. We should have called you Sparky. Do lots of animals here do that, Skut? I never heard of it before."

Skut shook his head, picked up the orange ping-pong ball and stashed it in his pocket. "Me neither. I'll have to ask my mother, if I can figure a way of doing so, without getting her suspicious." His face fell. "I don't know what to do about my parents. I wasn't supposed to hear that."

Podge didn't know quite what to say. He wondered if or how he could ask his father. But they were interrupted by *hungry.*

That made them both laugh. "I think looking after something that never stops eating is going to be hard work. I've got two more strips of patratti. That'll have to hold you till tomorrow morning. I guess we'd better go, or our parents might start wondering where we got to. We don't want to get found here. They'd lock this gate, most probably."

They walked back and in through the door into the

roofed over area. "So how does everything grow?" asked Podge, who wasn't much on gardening, but did know plants needed water.

"They sprinkle from the roof-pipes from two to four every night. Well. most of it. There are a few areas that have broken down, and have to be watered, like our garden."

They walked down the road until they came to a slightly dingy looking set of apartment buildings that went all the way up to the roof. "This is where I live," said Skut, awkwardly. "Can you find your way back to your house?"

"I reckon," said Podge. "It's only one road, really."

SIX

Walking to his new home, Podge had a lot to think about. The school was the pits. Well, he'd liked Skut and his Snarky…but he could see it would be difficult to keep Snarky secret and fed. When he got home he could hear Maddy had wasted no time getting back to her normal volume levels. He could hear her from outside the gate. She only had two volume settings, eleven and zero, and zero was usually only when she was asleep. She had some excuse, because she was making noise for two, as she had the mouse-like Pru with her, wide-eyed at Maddy bouncing off the walls while mother unpacked. He gathered they were 'helping.' At the moment, this seemed to consist of flapping two muffin trays next to her ears, and growling 'I'm the bat eared monster of the deep' with associated growls, while Pru giggled.

Mother was largely immune to the noise, and waved a greeting. "How was school?"

"Like school," he said.

"I gather from Maddy you wasted no time in getting into trouble," she said, lifting an eyebrow at him.

"Yeah. Getting a few things sorted out."

"Like what?" she asked.

"Oh nothing. Just some kid thought he'd push me around."

Mother looked a little worried. "You both seem to have had quite a day of it. At least Maddy seems to have found a friend."

He shrugged. "It's better than the camp. And I got on OK with the kid I had to sit next to."

"Skut. That tall blond boy. I have been hearing all about him. The girls are playing Skut's monsters."

"He's cool," Maddy informed them. "He's one of our armies."

At this point the conversation was interrupted with the arrival of Pru's mother, come to fetch her, and Podge got to slip away to his own room. It was a luxury after the camp, to have a room all to himself. He spent some time sorting his possessions and clothes into the right places. It was good, but it also kind of hurt. Last time he'd had a place for his own stuff had been before the Ghat invasion. Inevitably, no sooner had he got it sorted than Maddy charged in.

"I'm going to have to get a sign that says 'sisters keep out.' Go away."

She stuck her tongue out at him. "Mum says food is ready. But you don't have to come. I can eat all of yours."

That was enough to get him through to the dining room at top speed. She would have, too.

His father was looking grim. They'd learned to know

that look, and to worry about what the disaster must be. He told them. "Don't get too settled, kids. It looks like we might not be here very long. The only reason I didn't get fired today was that their water system hasn't been working for weeks and the storage tank is nearly dry. And half a dozen things are so badly in need of repair or maintenance that they could just collapse."

"What's gone wrong?" asked his mother.

"That auditor. You know, the fellow I met on the ship. The GM didn't know he was coming and when he went up to the Council office she refused him entry, saying his paper-work wasn't adequate. She came down to tell me, in person, that I was not to allow him access to the office, let alone the computer system. Only...he'd been already, and I had let him in, and logged him into a terminal. When I told her that, she nearly had a fit. Yelled at me for ten minutes straight. Told me I had betrayed her trust. She was spending serious money this afternoon, sending coded messages to some firm of lawyers on Ivory. I found my terminals are locked out of their main system." He looked at Podge. "I might need you to hack that open again for me, son. The water and power system are on their server."

"Sure," said Podge. "This evening if you like."

His father nodded. "The auditor left with the ship, so she might cool down. Or I might lose my job. It's going to knock us back," he said glumly. "Not that the job is anything like what I thought it was going to be. How was the hospital, Mary?" Mother had taken a morning shift at the hospital. She was a nursing sister.

"Pleasant enough. The younger of the two doctors is quite sensible. The older one is lazy, but it's well organized and the director knows her stuff. But, well, it's not going to break my heart to move."

"I just made a friend," said Maddy. "And she's relying on me, Dad! There's a nasty boy and his friends that pick on her."

"Well, Mads, it is likely to be months, anyway. They were talking about some big tourism push, but there aren't frequent ships, and I kind of made it obvious that only luck had held them from disaster, so they would need to replace me. Meanwhile, I have more work to do than any one man can achieve, and I may have difficulty getting money out of the GM to pay staff. And it seems that going fishing is another dream. Charter boats only, and we have to be careful about money."

"Skut was telling us all about the fish he used to catch from the rocks at his farm," said Maddy. "And about the birds and animals."

"With the result that they've been playing monsters all afternoon. It makes me quite relieved you won't be going out there."

"No, Mum, Skut says it's quite safe, if you know what you're doing," protested Podge. "I'm sure if you can take us out the gate with Skut, he can take us fishing. Or his dad, maybe. He works on the charter boats and he's looking for more jobs, because they're not allowed to go back to their farms."

"Well, I don't know. That's why this place is roofed in and walled. It is apparently dangerous out there."

"But they used to farm on the various islands on this archipelago. Sarah Morton—Mr. Loper from the supermarket's daughter, and Maddy's friend's mummy—told me about it. Their family settled here before the hotels were built. They got a lot of local produce, once."

"You should hear the GM on that subject. It should all be tourism," Dad said with a wry smile. "Not for ordinary people, at those prices."

"Well, only the super-rich can afford the supermarket prices," said their mother, pulling a face.

SKUT HOPED for a meaty meal that evening, with a little meat he could take for Snarky, but supper was long on Papa's veggies. His parents were being very careful not to let on that they were upset. They even asked him about how school had been that day. He hadn't even thought about it, until then. "Not too bad, actually, Papa. There is a new boy in our class. And he and his sister wanted to know about fish. No one else ever does." He found himself talking a bit about Podge and his sister. It was easier than trying to explain to his parents that he had Snarky in his shirt. He would have to do a late-night expedition to fetch more food for the little guy.

He slipped out of his window, when woken by Snarky. The weird thing was it was pretty late...and yet he had to dodge two sets of people. One was Podge...and a man. If it wasn't for the man, he might have called out to Podge. Snarky wanted to fly to him. The other was a lot further on, near the posh houses on the ridge. The GM, and the manager of the Ocean-View hotel. They were so wrapped up in their argument they probably wouldn't have seen him even if he hadn't hidden in the bushes. They came past. He couldn't hear quite what they said, but the anger in the voices was clear enough. "They'll be a rich enough prize..." was all he caught.

Hurty, sharp. Snarky informed him.

"Nasty" said Skut quietly.

Nasty Snarky latched onto the word.

The trip was worrying, in a way. He did have enough food for Snarky for then, and the morning, and maybe for school—but he failed to find any patratti or other food he could add to his store in the fridge. And while his parents hadn't detected the expedition, he was quite tired the next day. When Podge greeted him with a grin, he yawned. That made Podge laugh. "Me too. I had to go and fix a whole bunch of stuff for my dad on his computer. We only got home around midnight."

"I know. I saw you. Snarky and I were heading to try and get him some more food. Only we had no luck."

"I thought I heard...well felt, him. What are you going to do?"

"Have to take a chance in daylight, I suppose. It's easier on the lower tide-tiers, but they're pretty dangerous when you can't see. Or I could fish off the point—but anyone looking out might see me."

"You said something about fishing off the jetties."

"We can't get there. Hotel security won't let us go to the upper level, and the lower level entry is locked."

"Well...I have a pass-key. I was re-programming stuff for my dad, last night, and there were pass-keys, so I programmed a universal one. It'll open any door. I can do it through the door keypads too. But...I don't have any fishing gear."

"Don't need much," said Skut, beaming. "You can catch

tide-hoppers on a piece of string and a bent pin. You don't even need the bent pin much. Glass-fish you can scoop up with anything except your hands, because they bite. After school, OK?"

"If we can stay out of detention."

"Now I finally have a good reason," said Skut. "Stop tickling, Snarky."

Not even being told by the Vulture that the class project was to make a soft toy and that it was a team project, and that he and Podge would have to do it as a twosome because the girls didn't want to be on their team—a good thing, in Skut's opinion—made him less cheerful.

It was apparent that the means girls club and their hanger's on had decided to make things as hard in class as possible—like that changed anything—and to hold off on beating up Podge, for now. It was likely that they had got a bit of a fright at Podge not being the pushover they thought. He was mildly disgusted at having to make a soft toy, like he was three or something. The girls were all excited about it.

"So, what you going to make, pink undies? A rag doll? You can just use your clothes. We're doing a unicorn, and don't you dare copy us."

"We're doing a dragon," Podge informed her. "The kind that eats unicorns."

Of course, that led to: "Miz! The boys are being mean to us!"

But fortunately, the teacher was busy talking on the internal telephone system just then, and Jaccie had to settle for stating, "You stinky boys can't make anything as well as we do," as she stalked off.

"A dragon. How are we going to make a dragon?" demanded Skut, as soon as she was out of earshot.

"Well, we could always enter Snarky. He looks a bit like a dragon."

Dragon. Like dragon.

"I guess we'll have to do something," said Skut.

"I think I've got a hood with fake fur trimming. It's white, but we could color it blue."

At the lunch recess, Podge handed him a small plastic bag. "To put any meat in."

Skut had to laugh. "Better than my sleeve. Snarky licked it clean, mostly. But it still felt pretty gross."

However, there was a shortage of meat in the vegetarian meal the kids were served. It wasn't popular with anyone, let alone Snarky. Skut read the signs and hurried Podge and the inevitable Maddy and her little friend out. "There'll be a food fight. And if I am there, I'll get blamed."

He was right, too. The plan to leave for their fishing expedition was thwarted by Podge being reminded by Maddy that mother had found out that older siblings were allowed to walk the younger ones' home, and that he was doing that, and Pru's mother had sent permission for her to go with them. They had to be walked to Loper's, where Maddy was scheduled to go and play. "Sisters are a pain," grumbled Podge.

"If we walk past my place, I can pick up some line. I had a handline in my pocket when we had to leave Faraway in a hurry," said Skut. "Then we just need something shiny. They'll bite on anything shiny or moving."

Podge felt in his jacket's bulgy pockets, and Skut was taken aback at what came out. It looked like half an electronics shop. Bits of circuit board, resistors, bits of cable, several cogs, and things Skut didn't recognize. "Junk from dad's work. There were a few machines that had been scrapped. Dad said I could have the bits to build robots with."

"Cool!"

SEVEN

Podge was pleased that Skut was interested in the robot-building, but he didn't seem to get that Podge planned to make them work, not just play with the bits. Skut might know fishing and other stuff, but Podge had something to teach him about mechanical engineering and electronics.

Having dodged the food-fight made it possible to leave the school without running the gauntlet of their collection of enemies—as several of them were, to Skut's obvious delight, enjoying after-school detention. Maddy was more disappointed in having missed what been just her idea of fun. They walked along to Skut's rather dingy apartment block, where he was hailed by the tallest, blond bearded man that Podge had ever seen. The man was working in a little garden that you could barely see from the road, between the apartments and the wall. It was, Podge thought, the neatest garden he'd ever seen. Everything looked like it was standing to attention. A weed wouldn't have dared grow there. There seemed to be everything from tomatoes to beans, all in a little piece of land the size of his parents' new lounge. Of course, Maddy had to ask him why?

"Because it is all the land I have," said Skut's father, smiling at her.

Little Pru, who never said anything much above a whisper, said: "It's beautiful!"

She was sort of right, Podge had to admit. It certainly pleased Skut's father to have it said. He beamed. "I like to make things grow. I like them to be neat. Here, would you like to try my peas? You pick the pod like this, and out pop the peas into your hand. Then you eat them.

"Don't you have to cook them?" asked Maddy, as Pru tried it.

"Not when they are this young and fresh. Here, try one."

"I don't really like peas," Maddy said.

"These," Pru announced, "are the bestest thing I have ever eaten. You must try them, Maddy."

Warm and *hungry*

"I'll just go and grab it, Podge," said Skut. "I won't be a moment. I'm going with Podge, Papa."

"Good, good," said Skut's father. "You have fun, boy."

He pulled up little carrots and washed them off and offered them to the others. Not really knowing how to say no, they all munched carrots as they walked on. "Sorry," said Skut, awkwardly. "My father loves his garden."

"Actually," said Podge. "These carrots...I don't usually like carrots much, but these are very sweet."

They dropped the girls off at the shop, and walked on down towards the two hotels. Between them, on the other side of the main lobby was a series of smaller doors and ramps. "I looked at the town plan. One of those should be called 'vehicle access.'"

Skut nodded. "Over there."

Looking around, to make sure they weren't being watched, they walked across past the bins and skips, and to the pass-key door. Podge's keycard opened it and they were able to walk down the stairs, to the lower jetties. These were below the main tourist ones, narrow, and not built to be pretty—just functional. The water plainly washed over them when the tide was full, but at low-water they could still have boats tie up here. It was rather dim and cavernous, with the wider jetties above, but plainly a delight to Skut. "I reckon you can come out and fly, Snarky."

Snarky did, but promptly informed them *hungry.*

"We'll see what we can catch you, Snarky."

But Snarky had other ideas. He winged over the edge and dived—and flew out with a little fish—long and thin and wriggling. *Food!*

And then he surprised them both by dropping it onto the ground in front of them. *Eat!*

"Hey, you first," said Skut to Podge, grinning.

"I had a carrot," protested Podge, holding his hands out, defensively.

"Tide-eel is tasty," said Skut. "But watch out, they bite."

"Er. I think I'd prefer them cooked," said Podge.

"But they're tender and sweet when they're fresh."

Podge wasn't entirely sure that his friend was joking either. "You first."

"I think Snarky wants us to share his food," said Skut, and Podge realized that he was serious.

"But...it's raw."

"It won't kill us," said Skut, "Come on. It's important to Snarky."

Family

Podge swallowed. "I don't think I can."

"Of course you can," said Skut, taking out a knife, grabbing the little fish and cutting its head off then pulling the guts and gills out, like he'd done it a thousand times before. He probably had, Podge realized. He cut it in three little pieces, maybe an inch long. He picked up and ate the tail-piece, while Podge looked on in horrified fascination.

Skut family, approved Snarky. *Good.*

So, Podge had to brave it. He tried not to chew and swallowed, hoping it would not come up instead of going down. Down won...mostly. But he was rewarded by Snarky head-butting against his chin. *Family,* and eating the other third with obvious delight.

"Yeah," said Podge wondering if he would still throw up. "Let's do what we came for, Skut."

They took the head and guts of the tide-eel and Skut threaded it onto the hook on the hand-line. He unwound the line a bit on the jetty, and gave the line to Podge. "Here. They often hit while it sinks."

He tossed the bait into the water, and Podge found out hard that Skut hadn't been joking. The fish nearly pulled him over the edge with the sudden, savage take. Only Skut catching his arm stopped him. Then the two of them hauled furiously at the line, with *FOOD!* in their heads. It was quite a struggle, but they pulled a long silver and greenish-yellow fish onto the jetty. The fish was snapping, with huge teeth and writhing all over the place. And then Snarky dived on it, and there was a massive spark and a sharp smell of ozone. *Family hunt good* Snarky announced at the suddenly stilled fish.

"It's a good size," said Skut, plainly pleased.

"It is just HUGE!" Podge beamed, entirely forgetting the raw fish.

"Well, Tark can get about twice that size. And we're kind of lucky the rip-fish or Sarba didn't get it. They're always likely to snatch anything you take that long to get out. And a Sarba could eat it whole."

Podge swallowed. "Now I kinda want to catch one, but I also don't."

"Well, I don't," said Skut. "If it didn't bite the tackle off, which it is supposed to, and we got it up here, I think Snarky would have trouble with it. Anyway, they're all mouth and no meat. We'll go fishing a bit closer to the shore. It's deeper here than I thought."

Papa Snarky zap Sarba Snarky informed them with obvious satisfaction.

"He's getting up to four-word sentences," said Podge. "His vocabulary is growing."

"So is he. He's like twice as heavy. My mother says that all the Vann's World creatures grow fast, because small is dinner."

"Talking of dinner, do we have to eat this one raw too?" asked Podge, warily.

"No. I reckon we get to keep this one, and I hope two or three others, for Snarky for later. I wouldn't mind eating it—they're good. But nicer fried."

They got them quite quickly, and Snarky helped himself to several more tide-eels. Skut had plainly been watching the water. "Time we went, Podge. The tide is coming on. This place will be underwater soon enough."

So, they did. Skut had brought a carrier-bag with him, and they had four of the tark for future meals, and a well-fed, tired Snarky fast asleep. They walked out and turned into the circular road, which was where things went wrong. The mean girls table and their friends had just come out of the hotel, and closed in on them. "You smell of fish. Been dumpster diving again?" sneered Hillary.

Her friends all found that funny—and were closing in on them to surround them. "Just leave us alone," said Skut.

"Or else what?" said one of the mob, moving in and shoving Podge. Podge shoved back hard, sending three of the crowd falling into the bins. Skut swung the fish bag which smacked into two others. One of them grabbed at him, nearly pulling him over and then let go with a squall. "Run for it, Podge," yelled Skut, stumbling to his feet, pushing another kid away, and hitting another with a solid fishy thump. They legged it away. Well, Skut ran easily. The guy was built for running. Podge puffed along. He might have high gravity muscles, but running had always been his worst. Besides jeers and yells followed them, rather than the bunch.

"You OK?" asked Skut, like he wasn't running. "We can stop now." He wasn't even panting.

"Yeah. I hate...running," puffed Podge, coming to a stop and holding onto his knees, and feeling quite grumpy about it. He could lift and push twice as much as other kids. Why couldn't he run?

"This bag has a split. I thought I was going to lose our fish. And they're probably right, we'll smell of fish. My mother will go spare."

"Let's stop at my place," said Podge. "I'll grab you another bag and you can wash up. My mum is pretty unfazed by dirt and smells. She's a nurse, and we have Maddy in the house."

He over-rode Skut's protests and shepherded him into their new home and his room, which had a bathroom attached. "We can let Snarky have a fly-around." This proved a winner, but nearly got them caught, because they were laughing too much at Snarky and the ping-pong ball game to hear Podge's mum knock. Fortunately, Skut managed to snatch Snarky out of the air and hold him behind his back. "You sound like you're having fun," she said. "I have cookies and juice for you two."

She sniffed. "Fish?"

"We'll be right down, Mama."

She sniffed again. "Wash first."

"Thank you. But I can't eat your food!" protested Skut.

"Why not?" asked his mother.

"It...it would be inconsiderate," said Skut, awkwardly. Podge could sort of hear that he was repeating something he'd heard at home.

Mother smiled at him. "It would be very rude to refuse."

Skut looked confused. "Ah. I don't mean to be rude, Ma'am. But...but you need it for your family."

"We have enough," said his mother.

"Besides, your dad fed us," said Podge. "I reckon Maddy must have scarfed about twenty of those pods of peas."

"You got Maddy to eat a vegetable!" exclaimed mother. "That deserves extra cookies. Mind you, I loved popping fresh peas myself. Does your father sell them?"

Skut looked terribly confused at this. "No Ma'am. He just grows food for us. We used to farm."

"Aha. You are the boy from Faraway. Maddy was very full of stories about you, yesterday. Now, wash and come to the kitchen. I've been baking."

So, they did. Skut, Podge noticed, chose the smallest cookie...and ate it like a mouse. Mum was not at all like herself, and hung around them while they ate, asking questions. Really! Anyway, he quietly got another bag and went up to his room and sealed the fish up in it, before Skut could escape. "See you at school tomorrow. I'll bring that fur."

"Yeah, that will be good. Time getting there for just before the bell rings. Early and they'll be waiting for us."

Maddy got home a little later, as usual talking top volume, nineteen to the dozen. She was much awed by Pru's home. "They live above the shop. How cool is that? And you know what?"

"What?" said mother, moving the cookies out of reach.

"She keeps all her toys and all her books in size order. Even her dolls. On shelves. Like, weird. I think that's why Pru liked that garden so much. Everything was in straight lines."

"I wish you would put anything away! This was Skut's father's garden? I hear you were eating peas straight out of the pod?"

"Yes, and carrots straight out of the dirt. They're much nicer than cooked."

It was later that evening that Podge overheard his mother talking to dad about Skut too. "The poor kid looks half-starved. He would only take the one cookie, the smallest one, and he was eating it so carefully and slowly. Like he was savouring every morsel. My heart just went out to him, Rob. He has such good manners. Please and thank you, as if they were natural. He's a handsome boy too. I bet he has half the girls chasing him."

Podge rolled his eyes. Mum had no idea that yes, they were chasing Skut—to half-kill him if they had a chance. But it did make mum providing him with stuff for making the dragon—once he said he was in a project with Skut, very helpful, even finding some dye for the fur. "Blue? I've never heard of a blue dragon. Dragons are red or white."

"On Vann's World they are blue," said Podge, not knowing how right he was.

EIGHT

The next day Podge timed school just as Skut advised, arriving with his sister just in time to see little Pru with her hair being pulled, and a bunch of laughing kids tormenting her. Maddy waded in—she might be smaller than Podge, but she still had high-gravity muscles, and a temper to match her red hair.

Skut grabbed the hair-puller. "Stop it," he told the kid doing it, with the kind of menace that Podge expected the kid to wet himself. "She's littler than you."

The bell for class rang and they had to leave off, but at the first recess Maddy brought Pru along. "She's coming to school with us, from now on," she announced. "Her mother has to drop her off early to get to the shop. They bully her for ages before school."

"I suppose we could," said Podge.

"It is not that far from our apartment," said Skut. "I can fetch her, and we can meet up, come together. But her mother will have to give the school a note. I know because my friend Bill walked the Hendrickson twins to school."

"Yay!" said Maddy. "We can have our own gang. The Dragons!"

Dragons!

"Why dragons?" asked Podge cautiously.

"Cause you and Skut are making one. Mum told me. So, Pru and I are going to make a better one."

Podge rolled his eyes at Skut.

When the two girls were occupied in their endless game of hopscotch with Maddy rules, Skut said to Podge, "We have a problem. Mala told me they'll be watching for us down at the hotel. That's their territory. They think we were raiding the dumpster for food!"

Podge grinned. "I'm ahead of you. I had a look at my dad's computer last night. It's got a map of all the gates through the wall. There's one behind Lopers—and there is one to the jetties from outside. Well. I suppose it was from the jetties to the outside. There is a big garage for the earth-moving equipment out there. We go out behind Lopers and walk back along the outside of the wall, in that gate, and we'll not be near the lobby where they were hanging out."

Skut considered it. There was more cover around Lopers. The shop had been there forever, even before High-point became a town, and they had the oldest trees. But that route was outside the wall. For him that was a good thing, but Podge wouldn't know a stinger vine from a pumpkin. He'd have to watch him, as well as himself.

"All right," he said. "But I'll have to teach you stuff. It's not real dangerous on the upper tier, but you do need not to be stupid, Papa says. And I only have one flechette gun, and only a few more mags of ammunition that I had on my belt, when we got ordered to come to Highpoint. Mostly, you can avoid shooting, but there's stuff like hamerkops that will go for anything that moves. They back off when you fight back, but they kind of keep pestering, unless you shoot one. They go around in fairs—like a big mob, and they can be pretty bad."

"Yeah, but it's not that far," said Podge. "And you can teach me stuff."

So, after school they went down to Lopers, with Podge's mother, who was fetching Maddy, and, by arrangement Pru. Maddy explained the morning plan to her, and that Skut had offered to pick up Pru, and then meet the other two. Podge's mother was also keen for Skut and Podge to come and work on their project, at her home. "Later, Mum," said Podge. "Skut wants to show me stuff. And you can't come with us, Maddy. Before you even start."

"Big brothers are the pits," said Maddy, pulling a face and sticking out her tongue at him.

"Now, stop it you two," said Podge's mother. It seemed to Skut that she was used to them arguing.

They walked to Skut's apartment block, where Podge's mother demanded to see the vegetables that had actually got Maddy to eat something that wasn't meat or starch. "Oh, my word...I would never dare show him my garden. This is an edible work of art! Your father must be a horticultural genius."

Skut found himself beaming with pride. "No one knows more about plants than my father. Mother says he can make rocks grow."

"So what do you do with the big rocks?" said Maddy.

"Oh, Maddy," said her mother. "That's enough. Let's walk on. I want to get home."

They found little Pru's mother receptive to the idea—especially when she learned that Skut was the boy from the garden her daughter had told her and her grandfather about at great length. "I'll walk her up there before work. Are you sure your parents won't mind, Skut?"

This hadn't been quite Skut's plan, but he shrugged. "Papa is always in his garden then. The charter boats don't leave until the tourists get up. He won't mind Pru helping. I usually do that for a bit, and sometimes mama too. If Pru doesn't mind, that is? Papa doesn't believe in anyone not working, I am afraid."

Pru clapped her hands with delight at being asked. "I suppose that answers your question," said her mother, with a wry smile. "Your father can always say 'no,' though. But I am concerned about this bullying. I think I'd better go and talk to the headmistress..."

"Bargen will just take it out on us. They're her pets," said Skut.

"Who are these kids?" asked Pru's mother, sceptically. "I'll talk to their parents then."

Maddy promptly answered with the names of the ring-leaders—even the mean girls and their friends from Podge and Skut's class. "The others just follow along. Or are glad that they're not being picked on."

Pru's mother was silent for a minute. She bit her lip. Then she said, "I see. Our business rivals, the Council bureaucrats and hotel manager's kids. I think I understand where this is coming from, at least. The kids are just acting out their parents' attitudes."

"You and I need to have a talk," said Podge's mother. "I think this school needs some intervention. Anyway, you kids run along. That is, Sarah, if you still want Maddy playing here? It sounds like she upsets Pru's well-ordered life."

Pru's mother smiled fondly. "Pru delights in carefully putting everything back. It's...it's a sort of game for her." She smiled ruefully. "Her father was an accountant. He was like that too."

Skut and Podge sauntered out of sight. Lopers had more vegetation around it than most of the town, and it was easy enough to slip in between the trees and to the gate in the wall. It was hidden behind a big shed, and was a full-size drive through, as big as the main gate.

Podge inserted the card and it opened on well-oiled rollers. "Someone has looked after this," commented Skut. "Even the main gate is worse."

"What do they use the main gate for?"

"Not much," said Skut. "They used to take tourists out of it for a short, guided tour. They take a truck to the garbage tip once a week."

"Well, there are tracks here. Like tank tracks."

"There's a couple of diggers and machines the Council uses parked in a shed out here. Oh well, we should see them easily enough. Now, you stay on the wall side of me." He took his belt-knife and flechette pistol out of the backpack and strapped it on. "Ah. I don't feel dressed without it."

Snarky emerged from his shirt *Watch. Nasties.*

As they walked, Skut talked about the various things they had to look out for. It was fairly safe along the fence—someone had plainly got rid of any problem plants, and made sure there wasn't much cover for big predators. They got to the door into the jetty area, and slipped inside. The road divided, one section going up and the other down to the lower jetties.

"Perfect," said Podge. "Like it was made for us."

Catching sufficient fish was easy enough, and Skut would have happily spent the whole afternoon there, until the tide chased them out, playing games with Snarky, but Podge reminded him that they were supposed to go and work on their project. Skut pulled a face, but they set off back with a tired Snarky sitting on Skut's shoulder, and occasionally hopping across to Podge.

As they got to the gate Snarky chimed in with *Warm. Close.*

There was no cover, and the gate started opening before Podge even touched it.

On the far side was old Mr. Loper. He fixed them all with a lopsided smile. "I run a shop, boys. There is a security camera on my gate. Now, come in and let's have a talk." He looked at Snarky. "Storm-dragon, eh. I haven't seen one of those for a while."

They were all too startled to run, but Skut's heart was in his boots. "Please, please, just let me let him go. He was only a little critter. He'd have died if I hadn't rescued him," Skut said, desperately.

The answer he got, was: "Good for you. My Sarah raised two spill-deer, a patratti that was the most annoying animal I ever met, and tried with a couple of injured birds. I was wishing little Pru could have something to care for."

Warm, said Snarky.

Skut felt his mouth fall open. Podge was quicker to

recover. "You're not going to tell anyone about Snarky? Gee, THANKS!"

The old man shrugged. "The wildlife grow up fast here, and go off back to the wild once they do, or at least all of ours did. But, young man, I am going to tell your father about you going outside the wall, unless you do something about preparing for it." He pointed to Skut. "He knows how to deal with the outside. You don't. He can shoot, you don't even have a side-arm."

"I know," said Podge. "But I need to help with feeding Snarky. We just go down to fish off the lower jetties. I can't get a gun like his. I mean...I had one on Metheglin, but I can't just go and buy one here. They'd say I was too young. And my parents would want to know why. And I haven't the money."

Old Mr. Loper gave him that lopsided smile again. "You have saved me a lot of sleep, young man, with your computer skills. And my little grand-daughter thinks very highly of both of you. Before the war, Lopers sold all the supplies to the farmers, and bought from them—that's why we made this gate and road. The first jetty is mine. The hotel one is over it. I give you my permission to fish from it, and go through my gates. I also will bring an old flechette pistol and teach you a little, tomorrow—before you go out again. You will only go to the jetty, only in daytime, and you will not fish beyond the third bollard. The bigger fish won't come in that close to the shore. You will be doing some computer work for me, yes? So, you have a reason to be here. And you and your storm-dragon can fly in my shed. It is not like I can get local produce to sell at the moment."

"Papa said you were a good man," said Skut, his voice

choking up on him. "But I did not know how good. Thank you, Sir, so...so very much." He felt like he was going to cry with relief.

The old man shrugged. "I am going broke, so I may well do it in the way I like. Besides, I used to go to fish there myself, sometimes. We just are too busy now, and I can't afford any staff. You can bring me a fish or two. There's a fridge-freezer in the shed."

"There will always be fish, Sir," said Skut, earnestly. "You have seen others like Snarky?"

"I was one of the first people on Vann's World, son, I went with a few of the survey expeditions. They're not uncommon further towards the tropics. You'll see pods of eight to twelve of them, usually. I've seen a couple of pods here, over the years."

"Pods?"

"A name for a group of dolphins. They behave a bit like them, the biologist I was with said. They work together to hunt, and spend a lot of time playing around. Anyway, I must get back to the shop. Go into the shed and put your fish in the fridge."

NINE

Podge thought he could get used to living on Vann's World, principally due to Skut and Snarky, and of course old Mr. Loper. Skut knew a lot about the place, the fish and the animals, but he was a new-born compared to the old man. Skut listened to him carefully too, he noticed. They fished when the tides allowed, Snarky flew and played ball with them in the old shed—which was pretty big—at least thirty yards long, and high roofed too. Mother seemed set on spoiling Skut. Well, she made sure they had cake or cookies every day. At school the 'Dragon gang' had so far put off any open attacks, although the teasing and jeers showed the tormenting hadn't gone away.

His sister had settled into a friendship with Pru, which Podge realized, kept her away from endlessly barging into his room. She was, of course, in a fair amount of trouble at school, because Maddy never could keep her mouth shut, but she was big enough and tough enough that she could deal with a lot.

Podge figured out that most of the bullies and their hanger-on crowd were either bored or preferred to be with the ones doing the beating and teasing rather than being their victims. He kind of felt he didn't have time or interest in that stuff. He was too busy doing real things now.

SKUT HAD BEEN a little worried about how his father would take to Pru arriving there before school. That, it proved, was not a problem at all. The problem was getting Pru to leave. Papa loved his garden, and loved to teach, and Pru seemed to get great satisfaction out of precisely measuring holes to plant things in, and other very ordinary tasks. It worked for Skut. He could do other things, and the kid's enthusiasm and curiosity about the process...it made you feel good. Even about papa saying that nothing was really more important than growing food, and her nodding, wide-eyed, in agreement. Maybe a little sister would be all right after all.

The next bit of excitement was a small ship coming in—quite like old times, according to Mr. Loper. It was en route elsewhere, it carried freight the agents had booked, and even a couple of tourists, who, while this was not their final destination, were happy to take the chance to go out to sea. Papa got two days of full-paid work, and Loper's got a load of new goods. Some of these were piled into the shed—and when he went there with Podge and Snarky, it gave him an idea. He knew that Maddy and Pru took turn-about playing in each other's homes, but that Pru was doing an extra session with

Maddy, and then would be going to help in the shop, she informed them importantly.

"Can you look after Snarky for a bit?" he asked Podge, who was throwing the ping-pong ball for the storm-dragon. "I thought I'd go and offer to help unpack in the shop. He's been good to us."

"Yeah," said Podge, struck. "I owe him for the flechette pistol, and teaching me. Snarky could hang out in the backpack."

Snarky can help too

Skut blinked. Snarky had gone from one word to two, to three, to three in sort of sentences, and now four. He also weighed twice what he did when Skut had found him, misery itself, on the lowest tier. "Got to keep you secret, Snarky."

Loper warm. Not nasty.

They walked over to the shop. It was busy, as it always was when a ship had come in. It took them a little time to find the old man. Pru's mother was busy on the till, with a queue, so no use in asking her. He was hauling stuff to the freezers. "We wondered if we could help," said Skut.

Mr. Loper smiled tiredly at them. "I can't afford it, boys."

"We don't want to be paid. Just to help. To say thanks for...you know. It means a lot to us," said Skut, awkwardly.

"We're pretty strong," said Podge.

The old man's smile broadened. "And quick too. But I employed a couple of kids just after everybody got called in from the farms. And the Council Social Officer came and fined me both for employing underage people, and for not completing the paperwork. And someone would complain, and I'd be dealing with that mess again. So thank you, but no."

Podge looked thoughtful. "Um. Sir, Pru says she's helping when the shop closes...could Skut and I come down then? I could get my mother to give us an early supper. She's been trying to get me to bring Skut over to eat for a while."

"Papa will probably be late back from sea, anyway. I will eat when he comes back," said Skut, awkwardly. "Please, Sir. My father says to always pay your debts, and Snarky and I, we are..."

"The son of about the only farmer who doesn't owe me money, talking to me about debts," interrupted Mr. Loper, chuckling. "Yes, yes, you boys can come. Come around to the shed at the back, at five thirty, if that is all right?"

Skut nodded. "I will just have to check with my mother."

Walking away, Podge said: "Why not just come to our house? My mum won't mind, really."

Not warm. Skut...not right.

They both looked a little puzzled. And then Skut laughed a little uncomfortably. "I can't really lie with Snarky listening in. See, Podge, we're very poor. And my papa says you don't take if you can't give back. I can't invite you to a meal. We have only papa's vegetables, many days. For you to eat raw fish...it was hard. For me, it was food."

Food is good and then *so is warm, so is family.*

Podge was shocked to silence for a moment. Then he said: "Sharing fish makes us family, Snarky?"

Family, Podge, Snarky, Skut. Share food. Brothers.

"So, we shared food. So that makes Skut my brother too, right?"

Yes

There was a pause from Skut. Finally, he said, "I get it, Podge. But...but my parents wouldn't."

After walking a bit further, Podge said: "Snarky, do you know what everyone is thinking?"

When you make noise with your mouth

"When we talk. Oh. Okay, so do you hear everyone?"

Hear?

"Not the noise their mouths make, what they're thinking. Like you knew Skut wasn't happy."

Can feel your feel then *but two times fly shed.*

"And can anyone hear you? I mean like you talk to me and Skut."

Can talk only to you. Can shout for everyone. Makes me very hungry. Goes further.

Between them they worked out that Snarky could 'hear' or talk to either of them, no matter how quietly they spoke, over about twenty-five yards, and could listen to others at about the same range. He could in need 'yell', but it took a lot of energy. He couldn't do it often without eating and resting.

Skut found his mother willing, when he tracked her down. "Lopers?" she said tiredly. "They are good people. They gave a lot of credit to farmers. I heard they were fair about it. Will they pay you?"

So Skut had to explain. His mother shook her head. "Well, if you wish to do it, my boy, you go ahead." She smiled again. "With the work his grand-daughter is putting into papa's garden, we owe them something. I wish I could do more."

"I wish you didn't have to work so hard, so much, Mama. I wish I could earn money." He'd tried before. It was why he had no trouble believing Mr. Loper. They had had a 'formal warning' visit about his working from the same Council Official.

She tousled his head. "It will be all right. Go and have fun. There is a little bread..."

Very warm.

"You eat it Mama," he said, hugging her suddenly, understanding Snarky. "I am not hungry. I will eat with papa later."

It was a barefaced lie, but he had been hungry before. And, as it happened he didn't have to feel hungry for too long. Podge's mother had decided that she was coming to help too, as Maddy had been nagging her, and there was no way she could say no, now that Podge and Skut were going. She brought a sandwich for him, which politeness prevented him from refusing. It was very welcome, so welcome that he had to steal off and feed Snarky a bit of fish.

There was a lot of carrying and lifting, but with all of them doing it the pallets of boxes were emptied and shelved with surprising speed. Pru regarded the work with great seriousness, but obvious pleasure—and suddenly found herself the person who had to tell others what to do and where to put things. Skut had to grin to himself. She could become quite a bossy-boots, here in her own place.

Maddy had been cautioned to be on her best behaviour and oddly was, as Podge commented to Skut: "She never puts anything away at home without being chased, and look at her here!"

Pru's mother was plainly embarrassed, pleased, and a little worried. "Look, I really do appreciate all your help. My father is too old for this sort of work. It usually takes us until two or three in the morning. But, well I am sure we're breaking dozens of rules, and there are always people wanting to complain. They think we're making money hand-over-fist like that lot at Weltz-Herros. The thing is, they supplied the hotel trade while we supplied the farmers and fishermen. We got left with a sack debt that the farmers can't pay. But the local Council bureaucrats want us out, so they look for anything they can give us trouble about."

"You should hear my husband on the subject," said Podge's mother. "I don't think we'll be here long, to be honest. The General Manager has taken against my husband and is doing her best to make his life difficult. We were promised a lot of things that just aren't true either."

"I believe you. But I must ask you to warn the children not to talk about this. Not to give them an opening."

"My two have spent a long time in a Displaced Person's Camp, Sarah. They know how to keep their mouths shut."

"My father says the boys are solid. He's usually a good judge. And Skut and his father have been very kind to my little girl. She wants to start a garden here now. We have quite a lot of land inside the wall. That's partly what the Council are after."

The work was well-progressed by a quarter past six, when there was a knock on the door. "No working," said old Mr. Loper. "Upstairs, all of you. quietly."

But the intruder was not the Council Social Welfare Officer—but rather Podge's father. "I read the note, and thought I'd come down to see what mischief you were up to," he said with a laugh. "I need supper, so the sooner I help you finish the better."

Very warm Snarky informed Skut.

He might be, but he was also very strong, Skut realised.

He might be shorter than Skut's papa, but was a lot wider. Skut could hardly believe it when Podge had told him his father had a false leg from a war wound—it hardly showed in his walk, and not at all in his lifting. The job had been going fast, and now went even faster. By eight o'clock the job was finished.

Old Mr. Loper looked at Podge's dad. "Your son tells me you are a very keen fisherman."

"Yes, but it doesn't look like we'll get the chance. It's fish off a charter-boat, or not at all, and I don't think we can afford that."

The old man smiled. "Well, maybe not. But you can catch fish from the shore, or the jetties."

"I gather those are the property of the hotels, and they don't allow fishing."

"Ah. But they are not the property of the hotels, or not all of them. We were the original settlers here, and the land inside the wall is all leased from us. The rest of Highpoint belongs to us still. It's a peppercorn rent, because I did not realise what they planned—but I kept a jetty for our cargo. It is a low-tide jetty, and it is under the hotel jetties, but it produces good fish. If you would be good enough to join us, I would like to cook some of it for a small thank-you. Young Skut can go and fetch us some from the fridge in the shed. I can't sell it here, but I can give it to you."

TEN

Skut ran off in a hurry. He could feed Snarky and let him fly around. He was sure that was old Mr. Loper's idea as well. He was, Skut realized, the kind of man who thought of these sort of things.

By the time he got back, they had all moved upstairs, to where the family lived. It was bigger and more comfortable even than Podge's family home, full of things that made him homesick—a sea-pod table, and many pictures of the islands and of fish. He found himself buttonholed by Podge's father. "Mr. Loper says if I wish to fish from his jetty, I have to hire you or your father to go down with me, until I learn the ropes. So, how do I get hold of your father? I'll probably need you to keep an eye on my boy too."

"Podge can look after himself," said Skut, faintly defensive about his friend. "He is learning well. But my father would be glad of the work, Sir. If he's not on a charter-boat. The tourists will be gone tomorrow, but he usually has a day's work, cleaning the boat after them."

"I'd still like both of you. I know, sooner or later, Maddy will demand to come too, and she takes a bit of watching. I gather Mr. Loper doesn't want this known, and to be honest our General Manager might give trouble to anyone associating with me, right now. It is an awkward situation."

"I can ask him to come to Mr. Loper's shed," said Skut. "Only...I don't think he has any tackle. Do you...I mean, fishing here needs strong lines and hooks. I only have one handline."

"I've been offered a loan of a couple rods and tackle by Mr. Loper. How about Saturday?"

"I will ask. It will have to be early for the tide," said Skut, thoughtfully.

"Early is fine. I am awake at first light, anyway."

Skut nodded. "I better get home now, my papa will be back from the boat and will want his supper."

"I WANTED that poor kid to get a good meal," said Podge's mother, when Skut had left.

"Well," said old Mr. Loper, "If it works out, he'll get a good supply of fish. But there is no betting on it. His father is a very stiff-necked man. If he even sniffs charity, he won't do it."

"Sometimes all they have to eat is the vegetables he grows," said Podge. "That's why I asked you to do this, dad. Please."

The fish was excellent, meaty and flavourful.

SKUT FOUND his father had just got home. His mother was out. She'd left a note saying she'd got a little extra work, packing shelves at Weltz-Herros.

"My family. Shelf-packing for the rich. And they would not even let me bring bait from the Charter," said his father with a sigh.

"Well, Papa, I don't think Mr. Loper is rich. He works at packing the shelves himself."

"He is not so bad, maybe," admitted his father.

"He says that he's going broke. Many farmers owe him."

"Ja. He used to let them buy on credit. And now they cannot pay. I just wish your mama did not have to work for these people. But I cannot find more work," he said, with a sigh.

"Well, Papa, I have found a small job for you," said Skut, warily.

His father smiled. "Good. Doing what, son?"

"Being a fishing guide for Mr. Greene."

"Oh. And who is Mr. Greene?"

"He is my friend Podge's father. The new Town Engineer."

His father's face set like flint. "I do not work for this Town Council. They are thieves."

For the first time in his life, Skut lost his temper with his father. "Mama is stacking shelves at nine o'clock at night!" he shouted. "She is always tired. She needs good food. If they would let me work I would take any job! And Podge's father is in trouble with the General Manager. This is not for the Council. He doesn't like them any more than you do. He had to take this job to get out of the displaced persons camp. And he thinks he is going to be fired. He is a good man, Papa. I liked him. You can't..." He drew breath to start shouting again.

Hurt

"Huh..." He let his breath out in a big huff. It had hurt him too. Tears sprung to his eyes. "I...I am sorry, Papa," he said. awkwardly, quietly.

His father stood, silent, for a long time. Then he sighed. "I am sorry son. I too am worried. And," he said, pausing, "Too proud."

"I am proud too, Papa. Proud of you. I didn't mean..."

"Yes, son," said his father. "But you are right. What is this work? I will at least speak with the man. They are talking of putting the rents up again, now that the hotels are opening up."

Knowing just how hard it already was, Skut was horrified. "Come. We will walk to see him, Papa. I have explained it badly."

His father let him take him by the arm and lead him out. "He wants a guide?" he asked. "I don't think the charter captain will let him take his own. They charge the client, and they pay the guide. Besides it is not people like me. It is people like Orstrand. He is smart dressed, talks a lot."

"You know ten times as much, Papa," said Skut, knowing this to be true.

That did bring a small smile back to his father's face. "He does ask me questions, Ja. But he is only for the very rich."

"Podge's father is not very rich. Anyway, I will let him explain."

They walked on, and round to the side door of the shop.

His father sniffed as Skut knocked. "I smell fish. It smells Tark being fried."

Skut smiled. "Yes. That is what this is about."

The door opened, and Skut looked into the face of old Mr. Loper. "I have brought my father to talk to Mr. Greene, Sir."

"Come in, both of you. We'll cook some more fish."

Skut was not able to listen to his father and Podge's father talking. But of course, Snarky was. *Careful. Both.*

A little later, he said: *Warm. Good*

Indeed, looking across Skut could see his father starting to smile. Podge had been sent to fetch more fish, and Maddy was already demanding that Skut take her fishing. "Podge says I wasn't to nag. But I'm not nagging, just asking."

"It will be up to your father, and mine," said Skut.

"We can go after school. While they're at work," Maddy pleaded.

At this point Podge came back, carrying two more Tark. "We'll have to catch some more, Skut."

"I knew you'd been fishing before," said Maddy, triumphally. "So, you'll have to take me."

Fortunately, Skut was able to distract his father into fileting them—and then cooking them. There was even enough to take a portion home for Mama. Skut was pleased he'd fed Snarky before walking home, earlier, because they'd eaten almost everything in the shed fridge. On the way back to the apartment, Skut's father started whistling. And then stopped. "Sorry. Next thing they will think I have been drinking. You were right, son. I like the man. I did not know what trouble the Lopers are in. And I can get some decent food for my family. Robert...your friend's father, wants to go fishing to feed his family too. Oh, he likes to fish, but the prices that food costs...he knows that the General Manager wants him fired, and they must have enough money to get off-world, otherwise they are stuck like us. They would lose the house that comes with the job, even if his wife still has work at the hospital. She saw your mama when she went in for her check-up yesterday. She told me Mama needs protein...and now we have it. Did you know this Council health officer will not let Loper sell local produce? Because there is no approved processor to certify it! But the hotels will cook the fish from the Charter boats. Fish I clean myself on the boat is magically different from fish I clean myself for Mr. Loper to sell. Ha!"

"Why do they do that, Papa?"

His father shrugged. "We have less than one thousand people here. They have twenty people in their Council office. Not enough work, too much power, and a bad leader. It's why I like to be far from them. But now at least I get to go fishing. I hate to take money from Robert, but he is a proud man, and said that he will not take charity."

Skut had to smile to himself. It seemed as if Podge's dad spoke his father's language. For the first time since Billy had left, he felt that he had friends. And better still, his father had talked to people. Because they were so poor...his parents avoided any social things. As papa said, they all cost. He knew his father particularly hated to be seen as struggling. But...they all were. That, Skut realized, was different.

Hunt together. Warm. Good.

And he understood too, from that, that Snarky's kind hunted as families—and sometimes with others. *Many.*

ELEVEN

The next few weeks were, as far as Skut was concerned, the best he'd had since he'd come to Highpoint. They still got laughed at, and the mean girls were plainly looking for an opportunity, but they had learned to stick together in a tight bunch. It also helped that Maddy was perfectly happy to skip yelling and insults, and go straight to punching the girls—and she knew how to punch and had high gravity muscle behind it.

His father and Podge's father had struck up a firm friendship. There had always been enough vegetables to eat, but now there was plenty of fish too. The only downside seemed to be that his body decided it was time to grow. His clothes were all a bit small and tight now. Snarky was growing too. Snarky didn't need to eat so often—but he ate more. It was easier to feed him, if he didn't feed himself. The drawback was that there was more of him. Skut was glad to use one his father's old shirts that at least had space for both of them. Snarky also spoke more, and was getting some idea of what human words meant. The other thing he could do, now, was generate a truly massive shock from his wing-tip fibres and tail. Podge, of course, had to measure it. Snarky was generating about 500 volts! It took time for his 'batteries' to recharge before he could do it again, but as they saw by what Snarky did to a Hamerkop that swooped as they walked along the wall to the pier, that was enough to keep most trouble away.

And then, with a few days to go to the end of term, and needing to turn their 'dragon' project in, things went terribly wrong. It was a faintly odd morning—a small ship had come in, showing that traffic was starting to resume. It was a passenger craft, bringing little more than the mail and a handful of visitors. There wasn't much in the way of cargo, so the excitement of shopping hadn't closed school.

For Skut and Podge it was the usual situation: the two of them were in detention, again. Crawf had set them some math problems, again. But he'd said: "I can't let you go early, boys. The head has a meeting and several of the girls are working on their project in the hall. So finish and find something else to keep yourselves busy. Don't make a racket, or I'll come down here and make your lives a misery. I'm going to drink coffee and mark workbooks in the staff-room, where I at least have a comfortable chair."

They finished off the math in short order, and fished the model dragon out of Podge's backpack so they could claim to be working on it. Podge had been trying to make the wings work, but while they flapped, they couldn't carry the weight. "I will have to step the power up a lot. I'm going to rig these extra capacitors into the circuit."

"We can do it tonight," said Skut, impatiently. "We're

almost free of detention. I want to try for skimfish this afternoon. But I am not sure they'll come that close to the shore. Put it away Podge, so we can get out of here when Crawf puts his face in."

The problem was they'd got very casual about Snarky. He'd been playing a game that involved tossing his ping-pong ball from his perch on the top of the art supplies cupboard, and diving on it—a game he could play for hours. They relied on Skut's keen hearing and the fact that Snarky could sense humans through the wall, even if he couldn't see them, to avoid trouble.

Only it didn't work when trouble came running in fast. Snarky dived for Skut's shirt-front as the door burst open. But he wasn't quite fast enough to avoid being seen by Jaccie.

"You've got an animal in your shirt! That's not allowed!" she squalled.

"Haven't!" said Skut, valiantly, as Snarky squirmed for space.

In answer, Jaccie yelled "Have!" and grabbed at his shirt-front, ripping buttons and exposing Snarky. And then she screamed and fell back with a crash against the desks, her eyes wild and frightened. "It BIT me. It BIT me! I'm going tell!" And she scrambled to her feet and ran out.

"I have to run! They'll kill Snarky!" said Skut, his eyes just as wild as hers. "Give me the pass-key card, PLEASE Podge."

Podge shook his head. "She ran to Bargen's office. That's between us and the way out."

Can zap them said Snarky.

"No," said Podge. "Quick! Hide in the art supplies cupboard, Snarky!"

"They'll search!" said Skut. "They're coming!"

"Not if they find our project!" said Podge, pulling it out of his backpack, and dropping it on the desk. He hauled out several bits of electronics and several cogs, spilling them on top of the model.

"But Snarky bit..."

"Shocked her," said Podge, as Jaccie, clutching onto Ms. Bargen's hand, and with a viciously triumphal look on her face came into to the room, followed by...a man they didn't know, then Mr. Crawford—still with a coffee cup, and behind them the girls who had been working on their unicorn...still carrying it, sequins dangling.

"What," demanded Ms. Bargen, in an awful voice, "Is going on here?"

"She just wrecked our project, Miz. And she tore Skut's shirt," said Podge.

"It's an animal!" squealed Jaccie, pointing at the very obvious stuffed and winged furry dragon. "And it bit me!"

The silence was broken by some sniggers from the mean girls.

But Jaccie had plunged in too deep to back off. "He had it in his shirt! And it bit my hand!"

Skut nodded. "I did have it in my shirt," he said. "We were practicing for the presentation." He pointed at the dangling unicorn. "They are planning to move theirs with strings. It's a puppet, Miz. We have one string to make it come out of my collar, and then Podge is working on making the wings flap."

"But she broke it," said Podge.

"But it bit me!" wailed Jaccie. Her friends were all laughing by now.

"Hush," said Ms. Bargen sternly. "The inspector doesn't need to hear your bad behaviour, unless you want detention. Show me this bite, Jaccie. If you bit her, boy, you're in trouble."

Jaccie, her bottom lip trembling, held out her plump hand. There was a little black scorch mark on the palm—no sign of a bite, Podge noted with relief.

"There! It hurt!" said Jaccie.

"Capacitor scorch, Ms. Bargen. She got a bit of a shock when she ripped Skut's shirt." He pointed at the electronic bits on the table. "From the motor I built for the wings. She broke it. It's going to take us hours to fix."

"Very impressive effort, Ms. Bargen," said the stranger. "Electronics are so often neglected in these small remote schools. Good to see it being encouraged."

"Ah. Yes, Mr. Vikram. These boys show great promise," said the headmistress, smarmily, like she didn't make their lives a misery.

He'd picked up one of the workbooks they'd had to do the math problems in. "Mind if I have a look? Paper, eh. I suppose that is the problem and charm of these remote schools. The inner worlds are all touchscreen, but I feel this does force the children to learn some fine motor control."

Podge nodded. He could see Ms. Bargen grimace. But the man just nodded. "Well, you seem to be up to speed in that too." He looked at the cover. "Year nine, are you?"

"No Sir. Year Seven."

"Well, well. A tribute to your teachers, and a very good effort this." He pointed at the dragon. He looked Jaccie and the unicorn up and down. "I thought it was going to be a mouse in someone's shirt. I did that as a schoolboy, and it got away in class."

He laughed, and Ms. Bargen laughed awkwardly too. "Er, yes."

He looked at the beetroot red-faced Jaccie, and the other girls and their unicorn. Raised an eyebrow. "Trying to nobble the competition, were you? That's not fair."

"They're very good girls usually," said Ms. Bargen. "Do fine work."

"Well, I shall be looking at their work books shortly. I have high expectations of their mathematics and science, given the standard shown here. Well, boys, Ms. Bargen and I won't keep you any longer. Good luck doing those repairs, and I think, for year seven you're doing yourselves proud."

To their absolute amazement Bargen smiled at them too. "Well done, boys. Now girls, off you go."

"Can I get some paint from the art supplies cupboard?" said Jaccie. "That's why I came. Ms. Sanders said we could."

Cold horror filled both of their bellies. But Crawf, who was obviously irritated by having his coffee get cold, snapped. "No. And you can have two hours detention for your behaviour, and for coming into this room without my permission."

"But...it's not fair!" whined Jaccie. "I..."

"Out. Not another word. You boys can pack and go home," he said, peering at the dragon, with a frown.

"Yes sir," said Podge, hastily, getting down to it.

"And take your pet out of the art cupboard, and don't bring it to school again."

They both gaped at him. "I'm not a fool, you know," he

said. "Also, I brought my hamster to school in my shirt. Not as bad as the girl who brought a kitten."

"He's a rescue, Sir. Just a baby. I have to feed him often," said Skut.

Crawf sighed. "How often, Harkkson?"

"Uh. He can go about four hours now. It used to be two."

Breakfast to school-end.

"Can't someone else look after him? Your mother..."

"I haven't dared tell her, Sir. They... they go off on their own once they're adult. We have only a few days to term end, Sir."

The teacher sighed. "You'll be caught, Harkkson. That girl and her friends will be hunting you. Can't you get someone else to feed it?"

"I'll ask my mother," said Podge. "She...kinda suspects already. Come on, Skut."

Skut stood up, unwillingly.

Warm Snarky informed him.

"You can at least let me see your creature," said Crawf, mildly. "I have no intention of betraying you boys. But you must keep it out of here."

They didn't have much choice. He looked curiously at Snarky, and Snarky looked curiously back. "Intelligent looking little creature. Your 'dragon' is a good copy of it, but not what the classical images of dragons look like. You'll lose marks for that."

"Don't really care, Sir," said Podge. "We can't get top marks anyway."

Crawf bit his upper lip. It made his moustache droop. "Yes. Well, I gather the inspector is looking at math and science standards. You boys have thrown a cat among the pigeons there. I enjoyed that. Now off you go."

So off they went. When they were safe outside, Skut asked, "Did you mean that about your mother?"

"Kind of a maybe," said Podge. "I reckon Snarky could wait in the shed, and we could take a piece of fish out to thaw. You could eat it later, Snarky. You're smart enough to do that."

Can. Don't want to.

"Yeah, but you'll be keeping Skut from trouble. You want to do that, don't you."

Zap anyone gives Skut trouble.

"Which will cause more trouble. We'll be there straight after school."

Like to be with Skut. Family. You too Podge

"You're making longer sentences that ever, Snarky."

Understand, now. We go catch fish?

TWELVE

Podge's father came home rather late that day. "Sorry," he said with a sigh. "I've just been taking a few steps. Mary...I think we need to pack up bug-out bags. I hope I am utterly wrong."

"What's up?" asked Podge's mother.

"Well...I saw someone. You remember the Ghats intelligence commissar on Metheglin? You know, the one who tortured the Pardue captives?"

Podge's mother shuddered. So did he. "I could hardly forget him."

"Well, unless he has a twin brother, I saw him today. He came in on that ship, and he was doing a walk-around with the GM. She introduced him as an investor from Ivory, looking to build another hotel. Rolled out the red carpet for him. She looked really rattled though. It was very odd."

"I...I suppose people can look alike."

"Maybe," said his father, grimly. "I suppose they can. I'll swear I saw that auditor fellow again, and another bloke off the ship that came in with that small ship both walk into the Council offices this morning—but that also seems to have come to nothing. He must have gone again, as quick as he came, odd. He promised to come and talk further with me when he came back, and I've been wondering how to deal with that and the GM." He took a deep breath. "Mary, a lot of people, including us, lived through the Metheglin invasion because they escaped to the countryside, and the city-dweller Ghats weren't very good at hunting anywhere that wasn't urban. Here...we're all packed in, and contained in the walls."

"We've got a good defensive missile system," said his mother.

"Indeed. IF they don't come in on a civilian ship. They did that on Prather's World, remember. Captured the ship, loaded their troops, and came in looking like civilians."

"Yes, but the captain and crew are much harder to reach now. And the codes for de-activating the missiles..."

"I know. But the Ghats just don't have the resources or the society to not go on with their raiding. I sent a message and a photograph I took to Lieutenant-Colonel Morgan...I think he's still on Ivory. He'll remember me well enough. I think we're being scouted, but maybe it is all in my head. I hope...I just hope he takes it seriously and can do something."

Podge was glad he didn't have to bring Snarky up with his mother to add to the situation. He realized he hadn't seen his father like this for a year. There was a tenseness about him that Podge didn't like and wanted to forget.

～

SKUT HAD BEEN FORCED to explain the torn buttons on his shirt. His mother had been very unimpressed, and made him sew them back on. She was all for going in to the school to complain, and it took considerable effort to persuade her that would only make things worse.

The next morning, he set out for Mr. Loper's shed, taking Snarky down there. The idea of being on his own was making him unhappy. He was sort of used to having Snarky with him. Plainly the little storm-dragon wasn't happy either. He insisted on being under Skut's shirt—despite the fact that both of them had grown, and it was a bit tight. "I'll be back soon. And you sleep most of the morning, anyway."

Sleep next to Skut, family. Safe.

"I know. But I won't be far away," said Skut, feeling thoroughly miserable about leaving him.

Walking back he met up with Pru and her mother heading for his father's garden. Pru was skipping along, quite a difference from when he'd seen her at school before she made friends with Podge's sister and started spending time in the garden. "She gets me out of bed these days," said her mother. "I used to have a fight every morning to get her to go to school. I hear you had quite an adventure yesterday with one of the girls."

Skut blushed. "Just a misunderstanding, Ma'am."

"I gather from Pru she's the Council Planning Officer's daughter. We have had trouble with her. Fortunately, they don't really have authority over us. But she's the one who got the Health and Safety officer to give us a hard time."

They arrived just in time to see Jaccie's mother handing over a notice to Skut's father.

"What is this?" he asked.

"Form J233. Notification to either produce a permit for these structures or have them demolished within forty-eight hours," she said.

"But...what structures?" said Skut's father, puzzled.

The woman pointed at papa's neat raised-bed garden. "That. You have forty-eight hours or the Council will lodge an order with the works department and have it demolished."

"It's just a garden," said Mama. "Many people have gardens. It is not hurting anyone, surely..."

"You didn't follow the procedures required. It doesn't matter what the outcome is, procedures must be followed. A complaint has been made, and now you have forty-eight hours to produce the permits required, or demolish these illegal structures," she repeated.

Skut noticed to his shock that she was smiling. She was enjoying this.

"We will appeal," said Mama, wiping her hands on her skirt. "You cannot do this. This is our food."

"Oh yes, I can," said the woman to the audience, which had now grown to include Podge and his sister. "I'm just doing my job. The papers have been served. You have forty-eight hours to have this mess out of here. Penalties will apply," she informed them, in a voice that sounded as poisonous as trumpet-plant venom.

And she turned on her heel and walked off.

"What are we going to do, Helga?" asked Papa, wringing his hands.

"We will appeal," said mama, angrily. "This is ridiculous. Many people have gardens. They do not grow vegetables like you, but they are gardens. Why is she doing this? Who could have complained?"

"Nobody complained," said Skut, slowly, heavily, his heart feeling like lead. "Her daughter...she got detention yesterday because...because of Podge and me. She...tried to break the dragon and got caught. I am so sorry, Papa. This is all to punish me."

"She could not be that childish and petty!" exclaimed Mama. "That can't be true, son."

"I am afraid," said Pru's mother, slowly, "She is just that petty. We caught her daughter shoplifting. It's not that they are poor—Council bureaucrats are very well paid, she was just stealing sweets. I spoke to her mother—that woman—about it. She shouted at me, and next thing they started harassing us. Fortunately, our property sits outside her control. But she threatened all sorts of things. She has too much power, I am afraid. She and the General Manager are very good friends."

Little Pru had been standing stock-still. "She's going to knock down the garden?" she said, her voice rising to a scream, before she burst into tears. Then she turned and ran.

Her mother sighed. "Going to her grandfather. She always does that when she's upset. I'm so sorry, Mr. Harkkson. If there is anything we can do..." she sighed. "I'd better go after her."

"I am going to talk to Dad," announced Maddy. "He's the works-manager and the town engineer. He won't knock down your garden! It's not fair!" And she too turned and ran.

"I had better go after her," said Podge. "But my dad isn't going to knock your garden over."

"He may have no choice, if he wishes to remain

employed," said Skut's father. "And I would not put Robert in that awkward position. Your family needs the money too."

"Yeah, well, my dad might just make sure the excavator and dozer don't work," said Podge, tersely. "I'll see you later, Skut."

So Skut was left alone, looking at his father's precious garden. "I am so sorry Papa. I never meant to make her angry. The other girls laughed at her. She is...just like this. Spiteful."

His father squeezed his shoulder. "We still have fish, thanks to you, boy. And if they let tourists in, surely, they will let us go back to the farms soon."

"They don't want us to," said his mother, quietly. "The Council wants to move that this becomes a tourism-only world." She sighed. "You'd better go to school, Skut. Papa and I will go to the Council offices and see the General Manager."

So Skut went off to school. For once he didn't have Podge or the girls, or Snarky. He suddenly realized he hadn't been alone like this for quite a while. Class was its usual medium to horrible self. Boring, with him thinking about what that girl had done to papa, and hating her, and thinking about what mama said about tourism. She heard things when she was cleaning places. That upset him even more. He pulled back into himself as, he realized, he had before Snarky, before Podge and his family.

Podge hadn't come in. The bell rang for short recess... and Skut realized he should have been quicker to get out. The mean girls and their muscle were blocking him in. "Your backup's not here, pink panties," said Hillary.

"Dumpster diving trash-boy," said another, shoving him.

"Just leave me alone," said Skut, keeping his voice even.

"Sure. You just come along with us," said Mala. "We just need to check on something."

They pushed and hedged him into the boys change-room.

"Jaccie says you have a furry animal under your shirt. Take it off," Warren ordered.

Podge would probably have given a smart answer, but Podge wasn't here. So Skut just said "No."

"Come on, or we'll take it off for you," said Warren, turning to the big, slow Fred, who usually followed him around.

Skut was on the edge of saying "Try," but then he thought of all the trouble he'd brought on his family last time. So, he said: "If I take it off, will you leave me alone?"

"Yes. Once we see your furry beast. Show us," said Hillary.

"There's nothing to see," said Skut, unbuttoning his shirt, very glad of Crawf's insistence that Snarky not come to school.

"Look at the skeleton," said one of the girls, derisively. "What scratched you? Jumping into a dumpster?"

"No, that was Jaccie. She always scratches." It happened to be true enough about the way she fought that it provoked some laughter.

It also provoked Jaccie. "Pull his trousers off! I'm going to flush them!" she screamed. Up to that point they'd been fairly quiet. And up to that point Skut still thought he might get away with no major damage. Now he knew that had been a silly hope. So, when Warren lunged for his belt he kneed him in the face, sending him flying, clutching his nose and yelling. Fred, his sidekick, swung a fist at Skut's head. Skut ducked under it, and punched back, and with a lucky hit, got the next nose. Battle was fairly joined, one of the girls grabbed his hair...but before the mob had a chance to flatten him, an adult voice snapped: "What is going on here?"

It was Crawf, and just behind him the Vulture. "Stand still!" he roared, as several people darted for the door. To Skut's regret, he saw that Jaccie and one of the other girls had squirmed past the two teachers. But the rest were trapped. "Just a joke, Sir," said Hillary. The others joined in, with a clamour of excuses.

"Quiet," snapped Crawf. "What are you girls doing in the boy's change-room? Kate, you tell me."

Crawf, Skut had to admit, was smart. Kate was one of the hangers on, mostly there to stop them picking on her. She wasn't very quick or bright, and couldn't probably think of a story on the fly. "Jaccie said that boy had a furry animal hidden in his shirt. We just wanted to see," she whined.

"I see. So, you decided to take it off him."

"He took it off!" protested Fred, holding his blood-dripping nose pinched between two fingers.

"Likely," said Crawf. "And that's how come the two of you got punched in the nose."

"They were trying to pull my trousers off, Sir," said Skut. "Jaccie said she was going to flush them down the toilet. I...I did take my shirt off, because they promised to leave me alone, if they saw I didn't have anything under it."

"I see," said Crawf. "Where is Jaccie?"

"She ran out," said a chorus of the girls, plainly thinking that had she got them into this mess.

"Yes, I thought she was the one who pushed past me,"

said the Vulture. "I can't think what has got into her. She's normally one of best-behaved girls in the class."

"Perhaps it was the inspector finding her maths so poor that she will have to repeat the previous grade," said Crawf. "Anyway. You two boys had better get along to sick-bay," he said to Warren and Fred. "You've got a week's detention all of you. I'm shocked and disgusted by your behaviour, picking on a younger boy. Harkkson, get your shirt, and come with me. I think we need to talk to Ms. Bargen. She's had two complaints from parents about bullying this morning already."

Now that it was all over, Skut found he was shaking and feeling that if he didn't sit down he might fall down. So, he sat and put his head between his legs.

"Are you all right, Harkkson?" Even the Vulture sounded concerned.

"Yes, Miz. I just need to sit down. I'll be fine in a minute."

"Did they hit your head?" she asked. "Honestly, those boys..."

There was an eruption of yelling and screaming outside. Crawf sighed. Took Skut's arm, pulled him to his feet, and said: "You'll be fine. Let's go and see what the next circus is. No shortage of monkeys, eh Ms. Sanders?"

"I can walk on my own, Sir," protested Skut.

"All right. Come with us, though. It sounds like a riot out there."

The riot proved to be mostly sound and fury. But it was a lot of fury, if a very little cause. Pru was half the size of Jaccie, but she was on top of her, flailing away like a not very effective but determined threshing machine. Jaccie was attempting to cover her face and roll away from the little, furiously screaming, terror. The scene was surrounded by a ring of kids adding to the noise…that suddenly melted away.

The combatants were separated—largely by Crawf picking up Pru and depositing her next to Skut—who instinctively put a hand out. She looked at him and grabbed it. "Hold onto her," said Crawf, as the Vulture leaned over the ball of person that was Jaccie, asking if she was hurt.

"Right," said Crawf. He pointed to a small boy, who had been quietly moving away, just not as fast as some of the others. "You. Matterson. What happened?"

"Uh. Pru was running this way and Jaccie come running out and…and they fell over each other. Well, Jaccie fell over Pru, knocked her down. And they started fighting."

Pru was crying and being patted awkwardly by Skut. Jaccie sat up and scrambled to cower behind the Vulture. "She's mad. She attacked me!"

"She's two grades below you, and doesn't even come up to your shoulder," said Skut. "You, Hillary, and those other kids torment her and the rest of the little girls."

"Well," said Crawf. "That was the substance of the complaint made to Ms. Bargen this morning, Ms. Sanders. And considering what was happening in the change-room it seems like it is true."

"But she hit me!" whined Jaccie. One of her eyes was swelling.

"I think you ran into Ms. Sanders' elbow when you ran out of the boys change-room," said Skut, feeling he was paying back a couple of years misery, as well as what she was trying to do to his father's garden.

"It does seem very unlikely to have been Pru Morton,"

said Crawf. "Perhaps you could take Jaccie Stronk to the sick-bay, Ms. Sanders. I'll take these two to talk to Ms. Bargen."

That wasn't going to go well, Skut knew. But when they got to the headmistress's door, he could hear a very loud voice giving Bargen Basement an absolute ear-bashing. It was Podge's mum, by the sounds of it. Skut now knew where Maddy got the volume from. Pru was still sobbing and clinging to his hand, as Crawf—listening to the noise from inside the office—stopped his hand, just short of knocking. He sighed.

"What am I going to do with you two?" Crawf looked at Pru. "I can't take her to sick-bay, that girl and the boys will be playing victim there. Take her home, Harkkson. You have signed permission to take her out of the school grounds. Or was that Greene? Well, it doesn't matter, really. You boys stick together, and I daresay you know her mother. You can have the rest of the day off to go and change your clothes and get over all this...excitement."

"Uh. Yes, Sir. She comes to our g...apartment every morning. Podge and I just walk the girls from there. I know her mother and her grandfather."

"Right. Off you go. I have a class to teach in five minutes." He cast a sidelong glance at Skut. "Are you glad you took my advice, boy?"

Skut nodded. "Very glad, Sir. Can I go and fetch our bags?"

"I'll walk with you and see you off the premises," said Crawf, with the hint of a smile under his moustache.

THIRTEEN

Walking down the road, with Pru still holding onto his hand and still crying to herself, Skut had time to reflect, and worry a bit about the kid. She seemed inconsolably miserable, and yes, he'd got the better of Jaccie and the mean girls for now, but they'd still be there tomorrow, and thirsty for revenge. And then there was his father's garden. He kind of understood that it wasn't just a garden, just food when prices were terrible. For his father it was his way of dealing with not having a farm, and not having much money coming in. He knew that other farmers had turned to drinking, and, well, that one man beat up his wife. Papa just...gardened harder. What would they do now?

But his immediate problem seemed to be Pru not letting go of his hand. "What happened?" he asked gently.

"I hate her, I hate her, I hate her!" said Pru, her voice rising with each repetition.

"Tell me about it," said Skut.

He didn't actually mean 'tell me about it', just 'me too.'

But she did tell him about it. All of it. From the misery of her father being killed, to being the smallest kid and constantly bullied and teased and not wanting to carry this home to her mother, to her utter rage at losing the garden. Skut realized he hadn't been the only miserable one at the school. "I just can't go on any more. I can't. I can't," she said. "I just want to go away from it all. Just go to sleep. Never wake up."

"Yeah. I...I sort of understand," he said awkwardly, not really knowing how to deal with this situation. "I ran away from here, because of...that sort of stuff."

She looked startled, "But...but you're so big. Where did you go?"

"Well, outside the wall," he looked at her and took a sudden decision. "See, I was not thinking too straight. I thought I'd go home, to Faraway, and never come back. Look —I'm going to let you into a secret. Just me and Podge know. And your grandfather. Promise you won't tell?"

It distracted her enough to make her nod and look curious.

"Okay, so we'll go to your granddad's shed. I want you to meet...my best friend."

"You have a friend in the shed?" she asked.

"Yeah. Well, it's easier to show you than to explain." They were near the shop by now, and he led her along the side of it, and across the back courtyard to the shed next to the fence. "Snarky. I'm bringing someone in to meet you," he said.

SKUT! SKUT!!

Skut found himself dived on, and Snarky winding himself around and around his neck, rubbing up against his cheek. *Missed you. Was forever!*

Skut couldn't help beaming. "Only half the morning. Snarky, say hello to Pru. You can talk to her too now."

Pru's eyes were as large as saucers, and her mouth wide open. *Hello Pru. Warm.*

She stared. "It...spoke...in my head."

"Yeah, he sort of does. I don't know how it works. Warm means he likes you. I rescued him when he was a baby. Only, I have to keep him a secret, because we're not allowed pets. But he's not really a pet. His name is Snarky."

She looked wonderingly up at the storm-dragon perched on Skut's shoulder. "Snarky. Snarky, you're so beautiful."

Skut was aware of Snarky walking down his shoulder, preening himself and spreading his wings and waving his tail. He grinned. "You're showing off, Snarky."

Am beautiful.

"Yes," Pru assured him. "Can I touch him, Skut? Please? Please, please?"

"Ask him. He does like being stroked. Sometimes."

In answer Snarky walked down his arm and onto Pru. She finally let go of Skut's hand, to hold Snarky in front of her and stroke him very carefully with her other hand.

After a while, Skut said: "Hungry, Snarky?"

In answer Snarky launched over to the little bowls set on some boxes, flying into a neat spiral landing, the tendrils on his wings flaring out. Pru clapped delightedly. Skut, to his amusement, noticed that Snarky posed, before informing them *starving!*

"You greedy thing. Have you eaten it all?"

Was bored

Skut got some fish out of the fridge, and cut strips.

"Here," he said to Pru. "He will eat food out of the bowl, but he really likes it if you throw pieces up in the air for him."

Watching this, with Snarky showing off, and Pru squeaking and laughing with delight, Skut found himself pleased that he'd at least got her distracted from being desperately unhappy. He just wished it got him away from being worried. Snarky, having finished the fish, settled on his shoulder. *Little one is tired.*

Skut knew he was being talked to, not Pru. Looking at her she was indeed drooping. Not surprising really, the kid had had a rough morning. He took another quick decision. "Hey Pru. Snarky normally sleeps now. Could you, um, look after him, and rest with him for a bit?"

Tired. Sleep.

She nodded. "Here?"

"No, I think you can take him up to your room. If you let him climb under your jacket, we can take him in. You can look after him for me for a bit. He'll tell you what he needs. Go on, Snarky."

The look that she gave him said if he'd asked her to feed Snarky her fingers, that would have been just fine. They went up the back stairs together, and to her bedroom. He pushed the door open—it was the neatest room he'd ever seen, toys and books all size-ordered and square. "Get your shoes off and lie down."

"Oh, I can't do that," she said.

"Yes, you can," he said. "Snarky needs a cuddle and rest. I'll go and sort it out with your mum."

Tired Snarky informed them—and Skut actually felt tired himself. Pru was swaying on her feet. Skut realised that yes, Snarky's messages did make you feel just like what he was saying!

Pru sat down on her bed, kicked her shoes off, then leaned over and put them precisely together at 90 degrees, and then lay down. Snarky snuggled up against her pointed chin.

So Skut went out, down the back stair, and round to the front shop entrance. It was mid-morning there were only one or two people in the aisles, and Pru's mother was organising a shelf near the check-out. Skut had been hoping to see old Mr. Loper, but he could only see her. She looked up when he came in, and said with some surprise. "Hello, Skut. Not at school?"

Pru asleep Snarky startled him.

He realized that the bedroom must be just about straight above him, and that didn't seem to worry Snarky's ability to talk or even to know someone was there. It put him a bit off his stride. "Uh. Hello. Er. No. Crawf...Mr. Crawford gave me the rest of the day off. Um. I brought Pru home, she's upstairs in bed."

"What!" exclaimed Pru's mother. "Is she all right?!"

Skut grabbed her arm as she turned to run. "She's fine! Really. She's fine. She's just asleep. She...she had a fight, and got very upset. So Crawf...Mr Crawford said I could bring her home to you. Anyway, I um, stopped her crying, and she's asleep now."

"Is she hurt! Who hit her? I'll..."

Skut could see where Pru got her sudden temper flare ups from. He held up his hands calmingly. "She's fine. She was just upset, Ma'am. And I don't think she got hit. I think she's given them a black eye though."

"My Pru? Gave someone a black eye? Who...I'll have to apologise."

"It was Jaccie. And she asked for it. She knocked Pru over."

"Oh. Pru was very upset with her. You say Pru's asleep?" she asked worriedly.

"Yeah...I think it all sort of wore her out. She cried all the way home, but...but I got her cheered up."

"What a good boy you are," she said smiling mistily at him. "I must go up to her. If only father would come back. He and Robert Greene went off to see your father. Pop promised Pru he'd try fix what happened this morning."

Skut bit his lip. And then took the plunge. "I...well, Mr. Loper knows. But I let her take my, um, my pet to bed with her. Please, I know I'm not allowed to have it. But she was so upset, and she just needed something to cuddle. So...I've left Snarky with her. He...he's harmless. A baby himself."

To his surprise, she smiled, understandingly. "The animal you have been keeping in the shed at the back. Pop said I was to stay out of it and leave you boys to your secret. What is it? A patratti? I had one as a kid."

"Mr. Loper said it was called a storm-dragon, Ma'am. He said you don't usually get them this far south."

"Goodness! What an impressive name. And your secret is quite safe with us," she said smiling at him again. "Now, look, I just must run upstairs. Could you stand here and push that little bell if the customers need me?"

He nodded. When she'd gone he said quietly: "Pru's mother's coming."

Was listening.

She came back quite soon. "You didn't tell me it was a

little fluffy thing. So cute! It looked at me, and then snuggled into her. She has her arms around it." She shook her head. "I've never known Pru to get onto her bed in her clothes before. She's very...precise."

"She was...like, burned out, Ma'am. Can I leave Snarky with her for a bit? I want to go home. I'm...well, I'm worried about my dad."

"Of course! For as long as you like. And...thank you, Skut. You and the Greene children have been very good to my little girl. And she quotes chapter and verse of your father."

"She misses her dad, Ma'am," he said awkwardly.

He saw her close her eyes briefly and little tears start in the corners of them. She wiped them away quickly and when she spoke her voice was slightly choked. "So do I. So much. But I didn't realize it still upset her."

"It does. She told me," Skut admitted.

"Well. Thank you again." She sighed. "I suppose I buried myself in work. Anyway, here comes Mr. Jones. Come back anytime you like. And what Lopers can do for you, and your family, we will."

FOURTEEN

Skut was quite lost in thought, heading home. So much so that he nearly walked into old Mr. Loper and Podge's father...who were carefully measuring his father's raised beds.

"Hello," said Podge's father. "My boy was here five minutes ago. You just missed him."

"Yes," said old man Loper, with a twinkle in his eye. "I think he's gone to my shed."

"Oh. I...I better go back there," said Skut.

"Just a minute," said Podge's father. "Do you know when your father is due back? We need to see him. We've a... proposition to set before him."

Skut shrugged. "He and mama went to try and get permission from the General Manager for this garden," he said, rather bitterly. "It's not right. He's being punished because the planning officer's daughter..."

"I know," said Podge's father. "My boy told me." Then he frowned at Skut. "What are you doing here, son? Podge told me you'd gone to school. He wanted to go after you, but Mary said he and Maddy were to stay home. She was going in to read the riot act."

"Um. There was a fight. Well, a couple of them," admitted Skut.

"What Podge said might happen," said Mr. Greene, a little grim. "He said they'd pick on you if you were on your own." He looked Skut up and down. "You don't look too much the worse for wear. What's the other fellow look like? Are you in trouble about it?"

"Um. I don't know. Crawf...Mr Crawford didn't think so. But the headmistress..."

"But you got sent home?" he asked.

Skut looked at old Mr. Loper. They didn't miss that look. "Pru?" the old man asked anxiously. "I didn't think she should go today."

"Well, um, she's home, and she's fine. They sent me to take her home. She, uh, she got into a fight too," He admitted.

That startled both of them. "Is she badly hurt?" demanded the old man, plainly getting ready to leave in a hurry.

"I don't think she's hurt at all," Skut said. "She was just upset. But she's fine now. She was smiling and laughing before I left. I'd better go to Podge."

"Ah. Here are your parents, Skut," said Podge's father. "Stay a minute or two. We might need your help."

So, he had to stay. Looking at his father and mother, he could tell that things had not gone well. They both looked grim, and a little beaten-down. His father greeted them, not even seeming to notice Skut was there. "Well, if you want some vegetables, help yourselves. I'll have to harvest what I can."

Mama, Skut could see was just too angry to speak. Her eyes were narrowed and her lips set in a thin line.

"We have an idea," said Mr. Greene.

"It's no good," said Skut's father. "They will tell you to demolish it, Robert. I can't blame you, but it is all so stupid, so petty, so..."

"Calm down, I won't demolish it," Podge's father said, putting a hand on his shoulder.

"But they will make you. They told us. They are going to make us pay for demolishing it! With what, I asked them? The Planning Officer said they don't care," Mama said angrily.

"Listen to me for a minute, both of you," said Podge's father. "You can't work against these people, but we can work around them. You said you had a problem with the building and the morning sun here. How about the back end of Loper's yard?"

"It is full sun all day," said old Mr. Loper.

His father blinked. "I could plant there... Start again, I suppose. I can rescue some plants, seedlings...but won't they just do the same thing to me...us, there?"

"They can't," said Mr. Loper. "It is my land, and their regulations do not apply to it. They tried before."

"And I hope you won't have to start over," said Podge's father. "I've just measured the raised beds. I am sure I can pick them up with the front-end loader without damaging them, or not too much, and then put them down anywhere you want them. And you can say they were demolished. They lose, but they'll think they've won."

The look on his father and mother's faces was priceless. His mother hugged both of the men, while his father shook them both by the hands, beaming. Then his father said, awkwardly to Mr. Loper. "I cannot pay much rental, Sir. I…"

"I'll take it in vegetables. I think you will need a few more beds, and you will also have to put up with my granddaughter wanting lessons," said old man Loper, gruffly. "She was very badly upset by all of this, so I said I should make a plan."

"She is a lovely child!" said mother. "You will make a bed for her of her own, Nils. Skut will help…" Then she suddenly focused on Skut. "What are you doing here?"

He braced himself. "Some of the older children decided…decided to pull my clothes off. They were going to put my trousers in the toilet. So, I fought and, well, they got caught. So…so I got allowed to go home. I don't think I am in trouble. The girls, the one whose mother caused all this, and her friends were all in the boy's change-room." He'd been lucky, the girls change-room was at the end of the hall, or they might have taken him there.

"You hit girls?" said father, horrified.

"No…just the two boys," said Skut.

"That girl deserves hitting," snapped her mother. "I am going in to complain!"

"Uh," Skut, said uneasily. "Pru did hit her. It was not me, mama."

They all stared at him. Finally, old man Loper said: "My Pru? Hit that big girl…the one I caught stealing sweets? Pru is half her size."

Skut nodded. "Pru got her good—gave her a black eye, Sir. They had to haul her off. She's like a little tiger when she gets mad. Um. Can I go and find Podge, now? Please don't take me to school with you, mama. Podge's mother went and yelled at the headmistress already."

"You can go and start moving pallets. There is a stack of them just where the beds should go. Put them against the shed," said Mr. Loper, smiling. "To think of my little one punching someone. Mind you her mother...she has a strong sense of what is fair. She had a massive fight with her teacher once." He chuckled.

"You go, my boy. Anything else Mr. Loper says he needs done, he must just say," said his father.

So, Skut ran. He found Podge searching the bushes behind the shop, white faced and panicky. "Snarky is missing. You haven't got him, have you?"

"He's safe. He's upstairs at Lopers, with Pru," said Skut.

"What!"

"I'll tell you about it. Come and help me move these pallets."

They did. At a couple of stages Podge had to sit down, laughing. Skut began to see the funny side himself. "They're going to be all set for revenge though."

"Yeah. We'll have to stick together," said Podge.

Come play

Skut hadn't realized they were 'in range' of Snarky. "Pru still asleep?"

No. Awake. Wants to put clothes on me!

Podge started laughing. "She has caught that from Maddy. Except Maddy likes to dress her dolls as engineers."

They went into the shop, and were waved upstairs, to where Pru had laid out outfits neatly on her bed, and was now attempting to dress the storm-dragon in her dolls' best clothes. You could see the storm-dragon really didn't know quite what to make of it. Snarky did like being thought beautiful, it seemed. He just wasn't sure about the frilly red dress. Well, if Snarky was a 'he'. Skut had just assumed he was. It wasn't easy to tell with the native animals of this world.

"They'll keep you warm, Snarky." Skut informed him. "They're not just for pretty."

Make hard to fly.

At this point Pru's mother came up. "Go into the yard and have a look at what Grandpop has organized, Pru!"

So, they went out in time to see Podge's father placing the second of the raised beds, now in the front-end loader's huge bucket, down with precision and care. Some of the plants were plainly a little the worse for travel, but the only person looking more pleased than Pru, who was actively dancing, and had to be restrained from getting too close to the front-end-loader, was his father, who was already pacing out where the next two beds would be built. "Well, I will look forward to telling that woman at the Council that she has done us a favour and made our lives better!" he said, beaming.

"You will do no such thing, my husband," said Mama, sternly. "They did this to hurt us, to show their power. If they know it did not work, they will simply try something else and maybe hurt these good people instead. You will tell her you have removed it. That she has made life much harder for you."

"I do not tell lies," said papa, stiffly.

"Then tell them nothing. She will come to harass us, and find it gone."

Papa nodded. "It is fair to let them deceive themselves, Nils," said Skut's mother.

Skut turned this over in his mind later that afternoon, walking home. He'd been sort of looking forward to telling Jaccie that her revenge hadn't worked, and his family were now better off. But Mama was right. Jaccie's mother would find some other way to get back at his family, or at the Lopers. Come to think of it, she would be pretty mad at them for what Pru had done to Jaccie. And they were being very kind to him and Snarky. Snarky had rapidly moved to being Pru's mother's favorite too. "I gather you can't take him to school, so you hid him in the shed. But it must be very lonely in there. I could make him a little bed in the office. One of us is usually up there. He is housetrained, isn't he, and he will stay there won't he? I don't want him frightening customers."

"Oh yes, Ma'am. He knows how to use the toilet."

Water with no fish was Snarky's rather disappointed reaction to the toilet, but he was good at using it.

That did ease a big worry about going to school and leaving Snarky. And, well, his parents were a lot more food secure than they had been. Papa could—and would—produce a lot of excess fresh produce with a bit more space and sun, and they had fish, now. But he was still wary about what going to school would bring them, the next day.

As it worked out, it was not at all what he'd feared. Bargen called them all to an assembly that morning, read a long, boring lecture about bullying and acceptable behavior, and warned of serious consequences if there were any more incidents. They filed off to class, and got in before the Vulture. Jaccie was sporting a magnificent black eye, and looking as angry as if she had her own storm cloud hanging over her.

Podge, of course, could not resist. "Nice eye makeup, Jaccie. Are you allowed to wear it to class?"

"This is all your fault, you horrible dumpster diving boys! You did this to make me look stupid!"

Podge snorted. "No, that's something you do without any help, Jaccie." That got some laughter.

Skut, thinking about what his mother had told his father said: "Ease up, Podge. Let her be, please."

Far from helping, that just made Jaccie turn on him. "You just wait," said Jaccie. "My mother's going to get you evicted because your father broke Council rules."

"The garden got dug up yesterday," said Podge.

"Yes," said Skut, his blood cold with rage, and fear too. There would be nowhere for them to go. "Your mother gave us two days to dig up my father's vegetable garden. He did it."

"I hope you're happy," said Podge. "That was their food."

Skut decided that it didn't matter if his father wasn't going to lie. He'd just have to do his best. "It's expensive and hard here. I do not know how my parents manage. The garden helped a little. My mother is pregnant and needs good food," he said, loudly, clearly, and coldly.

There was an audible intake of breath from several people. But just at this point the Vulture came in and set them to work. For once she didn't seem to be spending her time picking on Podge or Skut, but actually gave the mean girls a rocket for their usual talking and note passing.

At first recess they got out of classroom quickly, and made their way to their usual bench, to be joined by Maddy and Pru...and four other kids. "They want to join our gang," Maddy informed the boys. "Because Pru will protect them from the big kids." Skut wasn't entirely sure if it was a joke, or whether he and Podge were now the guardians. Pru was still undoubtably the littlest of them, but no longer the shyest. It was quite interesting to see that she had now taken over as chief organizer of the hopscotch. They were noisy and cheerful, and it helped to lift Skut's mood. He was still worried about Jaccie's latest threat, though.

At second recess they sat down at their usual table in the awkward-to-get-to corner in the cafeteria, when a group of three girls from their own grade came across to the table. "Mind if we sit down?" said one, in a carefully neutral voice.

"Can't stop you," said Podge, warily.

They did. Kate, the one who sometimes ran with the mean-girls as a sort of camp-follower, had no sooner sat down, when she asked: "Is that, like, true about your vegetable garden being demolished on Jaccie's mother's orders?

"Yeah," said Skut. "Ask Podge. Or the girls. They were there." He was glad that he'd been able to tell Maddy and Pru not to give away what had actually happened to the raised beds.

"And she's threatening to have you kicked out of your home when your mum is going to have a baby?"

Skut was too choked up by that to do more than nod. But Podge said: "You heard her."

"I didn't believe it when she said it. That's like, so mean. Spiteful!" exclaimed Kate.

Pru stood up, her chin jutting. "I'm going to hit her again!" she announced.

Skut grabbed her. She wasn't joking. "You're a champ. But Snarky wouldn't like it if you got detention."

"But she mustn't do that!" said Pru stormily.

"I don't think she can," said Skut. "And hitting her again wouldn't help."

"And anyway," said Maddy. "I get to hit her first. It's not fair you got to have all the fun."

The group of girls had begun to giggle at this. "Don't let Ms. Bargen hear you!"

"Why? Does she also want a turn?" asked Podge, innocently.

This provoked more giggles. "You're funny."

"Not as funny as Vulture when she forgot her false teeth," said Podge, grinning.

"Vulture?" asked Linda.

"You know. Red claws." He held up his nails. "Naw naw girls, settle daan," he said in a credible imitation.

That was too much for the girls, who dissolved into shrieks of mirth. "You'll get into such trouble!" said Anne, the third one of them.

"Probably," said Skut. "You'd better cool the volume. I am in enough trouble as it is."

The rest of recess passed more pleasantly than any Skut could remember. The girls were more curious about Podge and off-world, but it was apparent that the tide of opinion had shifted—at least with them. Skut just hoped it didn't make Jaccie even madder, and more inclined to get her mother to try nasty moves.

It worried him. But that evening he learned that he had worried about the wrong thing.

FIFTEEN

Podge left Skut at the Lopers. Skut had taken Snarky in to Pru and as they hadn't—yet—let his sister in to the secret of the Storm-dragon. Skut was willing. Podge wasn't. The trouble was, he knew his sister. Oh, she'd keep the secret to death...on purpose, but she was as likely to forget and start talking about it by accident. She'd say the first thing on her mind, and think about it later. So, he'd taken Maddy home. Skut had been told by his father, who was working on the new raised beds, that he must be home by seven. That was just after dark, and Podge had been slightly jealous. He had to be home when the lights came on.

Podge's father got in, just at dusk. He'd barely said hello to them, when they heard the sound of a ship coming in. His father frowned. "That's descending fast. And nothing was expected until the VIP ship on Monday. I am supposed to make the town look pretty by then for the cameras."

He went out to look. Then came hastily back into the kitchen-diner where Podge and his sister were being made use of at preparing supper—peeling vegetables they'd got from Skut's father. "Mary. Kids. Get your bug-out bags. We're going. Move!"

When he spoke like that, no-one stopped to ask why or what. They did it at a run. A minute later they were trotting down the road with him. "What is it?" asked Mother.

"I think it's a Ghat ship." He reached into his pocket, and pulled out three gate-cards. "Now. If we're separated, head for the gate behind Lopers. And then go to the Mechanical workshop outside the gate. We'll stick together, if possible." He smiled wryly. "If I am wrong, we can always come back. I've changed the passcode on the gates, so they won't respond to the old code. They could blow it down but it will buy us time."

Podge knew the system well enough to know that the universal code-card he'd made for the gates would still work. "Can we warn the Lopers? Skut might still be there?" he asked.

His father nodded. "You go with Mom and Maddy. I'll nick in and tell the old man. He'd be an asset out there."

They hurried on. Suddenly, a booming voice came from what Podge later learned was a fire-alarm system. "ATTENTION! ATTENTION! THIS IS THE GENERAL MANAGER. ALL CITIZENS PROCEED TO CENTRAL PARK IMMEDIATELY. ASSEMBLE TO CENTRAL PARK. THIS IS A MILITARY EMERGENCY."

"Keep walking," said his father. "We only have seventy yards to go."

But it was seventy yards too far. A Ghat ground-car was ahead of them, disgorging troops in the black-and-white fish-net patterned uniform they had come to hate and fear.

"Stay calm," said his father.

"Go to the Central Park," said the Officer of the squad, looking at them. "You will not be harmed if you obey orders."

"Yes, Sir. Can my children go and fetch their grand-mother? It is close. We will wait here."

"No. Move or be shot."

"Yes, Sir. That is the shortest road there. May we take it?" said his father pointing to the avenue just ahead.

"Yes. Go," said the officer. "You three," he said to his men, "Remain here. Turn any more of the prisoners to that road."

So close...there were the trees behind Mr. Loper's shed and the path he and Skut used as a short-cut not fifteen feet away.

"We will have to take our chances when we get them," said his father quietly.

WITH NOTHING more than the weekend coming up on his horizon, Skut felt he at least had no worries until Monday. The Council offices were shut, and they were unlikely to do a stroke of work, even being mean, out of work hours. He'd been for a fish with Podge, and it looked like they'd have to take Maddy along with them tomorrow. Well, he could get Pru to look after Snarky.

He was in the shed, feeding Snarky, when the instruc-tion came over the fire-system speakers. He would have gone at once...except Snarky hadn't even started eating. Well, it would take even longer to get there for the people working in the hotels than from here to the central park, and when would he get a chance to feed Snarky again? So, he cut up some extra fish, and told Snarky to gobble up. "We'll go find out what is going on. Find mama and papa."

So Snarky ate up, and Skut tucked him in his shirt. It was a tight fit, but he wanted Snarky close. He locked up the shed, and began walking through the trees around the back of it—the shortest way to the road.

Podge said Snarky, as they reached the bushes and a vehicle came screeching to a halt.

Looking out from the shadows of the trees, Skut saw Ghat soldiers jump out of the troop carrier. He ducked behind the tree-trunk. But they were not looking his way. They were looking...at Podge and his family. Skut was close enough to hear it all.

For a moment he didn't know what to do. Then he said quietly, under his breath. "Snarky. Can you still talk to Podge? Ask him to ask his dad what I can do?"

Yes. Nasty

"DAD," said Podge. "Skut is in the trees, just behind us. He wants to know what he can do?"

"Wish we could talk to him."

"I can, Dad. But he'll be out of range in a minute."

"You can? Ok, tell him there's a fuse box for the power plant at the gate. Above the access key-pad and card reader. Does he know what a fuse box is?"

"He says he knows what you mean."

"Tell him to pull all the switches down. The street lights will go out. We'll try to come back to him, at the gate. None of the moons are up and it will be pitch dark."

"He says yes."

"Walk slowly. And hold hands."

It seemed a long time before all the light suddenly flicked out. Podge was prepared for it. He was not prepared for just how dark it would be. Or for the sound of one of the Ghat soldiers, now maybe forty yards away firing at something, and a brief muzzle-flash. "Can't see a thing..." said his father. "Well, neither can they. If they stay put, we're in trouble. We'll just have to go as quietly as we can."

So, holding hands and keeping as quiet as possible, they turned back. Podge could have sworn the Ghats would hear his heart pounding.

Slowly, not knowing how far they had gone, they made their way back along the avenue—using their feet to feel if they were still on the road. In the distance, Podge heard more shots, and the sound of vehicles.

And then *Podge*

"Snarky!"

Shsh. Nasty ahead. Stop

He did, squeezing his father's hand, hard. Fortunately, his dad got the message. They stood, hardly daring to breathe.

And then he felt claws landing on his shoulder. *Walk left. On grass*

So he tugged at his father's hand. And then again until his father, reluctantly it seemed, followed. A little while later they came to a low wall. *Wall* warned Snarky. *Crawl Skut says*

He pulled his father down. Pulled himself close to his father's ear. "Crawl. Skut says."

"Are the nasties close?" he asked under his breath.

More than two sheds

He translated that in his head. They were at least sixty yards away. Maybe as far as Snarky could 'see'. He knew where the wall was too, now. It was the back boundary to the property across the road from the Lopers.

Yes. Skut across road. Has gun. Tell father.

So, Podge whispered where they were, and that Skut had his flechette pistol.

"So have I. But I can't see to shoot. And those rifles have range on a pistol," said his father quietly. "And don't whisper. The sound carries further."

"They're more than sixty yards up the road. We can cross quietly."

They crossed, and Podge suddenly felt Snarky land on his shoulder, and a hand touch him. *Skut.*

Skut towed the line of Podge's family into the bushes and darkness.

Pru. Scared.

"Tell Pru we're coming," said Skut. "I'll get you guys to the gate, and go fetch her."

"I'll go," said Podge's father.

"I can see in the dark, sir. And talk to her long range."

A minute later Skut said. "The gate. Open it. I'll be back."

Safe outside. No teeth waiting.

They could tell where the gate was, by feel. It was still pitch dark.

SKUT LET Snarky lead him by pressure on his shoulder, back to the rear stairs of Lopers. At the foot of the stairs Snarky informed him that Pru and her mother were sitting on the landing. *Dangerous. Mother. Scared.*

"Tell Pru it's me. Tell her mum." Skut subvocalized.

"It's Skut, Mummy," said a little voice from above. "Don't shoot him."

"Skut?" Mrs. Morton asked in an uncertain voice.

"Yes, ma'am. It's the Ghats. I've come to get you out. Podge's family are waiting. Please come down, quickly. We need to get out of here."

He heard the stairs creak as they came. Then a reaching cold hand touched him. He felt for it and took it and led them away, as a vehicle could be heard driving closer, slowly. "Is Mr. Loper with you," asked Skut, suddenly.

"No. Grandpop has gone to the hospital," said Pru.

"What?" exclaimed Skut, alarmed.

"To fetch his blood-pressure pills. He does it every month," said Pru's mother. "It just had to be this evening. That vehicle..."

"Sounds like they're looking for something."

"Never mind, we'll be out of the gate in a minute."

Waiting at the gate. Podge.

Skut expected them to be waiting outside the gate, but they weren't. "It needs power," Podge's father explained. "And that vehicle...someone is probably looking for the power controls. If they're in with the General Manager...they know our SMNR unit is just outside this gate. They'll find the road soon."

"Well, let's turn the lights on again, and they'll stop look-ing," said Skut, practically. "Better than standing here."

"They might see us," said Podge.

"If they find the road to drive in here they will. And we can lock it behind us."

"True. They can knock it down, or blow a hole in it but it will take time. Okay let's go," said Podge's dad.

The lights came on. Podge was standing by with the key card, and they hastened out into the dark, as the gate closed behind them.

There were no yells or shots. After a few seconds Podge said: "Where do we go now?"

"I need to go back," said Skut. "To fetch my parents."

"Will you get my grandpop too?" asked Pru.

"He can't do everything, dear," said her mother, tremulously.

"Yes, he can," Pru informed her.

"He's certainly an amazing young man," said Podge's father, "but...well, could you get us to the workshop? We can talk strategy there?"

Skut was deeply relieved to do that. He was trying to work out just how he'd get to his parents, let alone Pru's grandfather.

The workshop sheds contained several trucks, the fire engine, the front-end loader, and a couple of electric quads and trailers, as well as fuel tanks and the tools for main-taining the vehicles. It also had a small office with a couple of desks and toilet facilities. It also had a hook-up to the PA system that broadcast the Fire Alarm. So: they were able to hear the General Manager "...YOU HAVE FIFTEEN MINUTES TO RETURN TO YOUR OWN

DWELLING PLACE AND REMAIN THERE UNTIL FURTHER ORDERS. THERE IS A STRICT CURFEW. ANYONE FOUND OUTSIDE THEIR DWELLINGS AFTER THIS WILL BE SHOT. FOLLOW ORDERS AND YOU WILL NOT BE HARMED. HIGHPOINT STATION IS NOW UNDER THE AUTHORITY OF THE EMIRATE."

Skut looked at the escapees in the little office. They looked back at him. "What's that?" asked Maddy, looking at Snarky, sitting on his shoulder, tail coiled around Skut's neck.

"A storm-dragon. He's a...a native animal. I rescued him. He can sort of see in the dark and stuff," said Skut.

"The two of you saved our bacon," said Podge's mother. "What an amazing little creature." She looked speculatively at Podge. "I see what you were modelling that dragon on. But what are we to do now, Robert? Are they setting out to conquer this world too?"

Podge's father shook his head. "No. It is too small a ship. It's a raid to take slaves and possibly hostages. If something goes wrong the Emir of Ghatistan will say that they're a rogue element. I think the target may be that VIP ship that was arranged to relaunch the tourism business. The Premier of Ivory and a bunch of ministers, media people, and influencers are supposed to be landing on Tuesday. They have value. The rest of the people...are slaves at best, unless they have rich families."

"What can we do?" asked Pru's mother.

"Survive would be the start. They probably won't stay long. The trouble is that there are probably—looking at the ship size—somewhere between two to three hundred of them. I imagine they'll round everyone up but leave a few to look normal and lock the rest of them away, so that the Premier's ship lands, unsuspecting. The only weapons we have are two flechette pistols."

"Three," interrupted Podge. "I have one that I got from Mr. Loper, so that he'd let me go fishing with Skut."

His father looked a little taken aback. "Well, three. And I see you have a pump-action shotgun, Sarah. But they're all close-range weapons and we don't have much ammunition. I can make some explosives with the fuel—but the Ghats are actually very good at urban warfare, and they have rifles."

The PA system crackled to life again. "ATTENTION. ATTENTION. ANYONE WHO KNOWS THE WHEREABOUT OF ROBERT GREENE, TOWN ENGINEER, INFORM THE SOLDIERS ON PATROL. THEY WILL BE DOING HOUSE-TO-HOUSE CHECKS. HAVE YOUR PAPERS READY, THEY WILL BE CHECKING IF ALL RESIDENTS ARE IN THEIR HOMES. THEY HAVE A FULL LIST. BEHAVE AND YOU WILL NOT BE HARMED. RESIST AND YOU WILL BE KILLED."

"They can be quite efficient," said Podge's father, grimly. "They probably wanted me for the power issue, and found me missing."

"I must try and get to my parents, Sir," said Skut, his heart in his boots. "If we could kill the power again, Snarky can avoid them. It's an hour to moonrise...but then I will be stuck inside."

"I had a thought about that," said Podge's father. "If I took you around to the Containment Lab door, on one of the quads, we could go along the track next to the wall. That door is much closer to your parents' apartment You and I…"

"No, Sir," said Skut, hastily.

"Why not?" he asked.

Skut grinned. "I'm trying to say this politely, Sir, but you walk like a Skarbin…um, something like an elephant. And you see, Snarky can see in complete darkness, and he talks to me, not you. Get me to the gate…and find me some way of getting back out, and I will do the rest."

"He's right, Dad," said Podge. "You can't do it without Snarky, and Snarky won't go without Skut, and Snarky can tell if there is someone even close. As for the power…there's a terminal here. I can hack the system, and leave the gate circuit live. Shut the rest down."

Podge's father sucked his teeth. "They're sure to come and check if we're at the power unit. And they might search here, if they see the place."

"Then," said Pru's mother, "we could go up to my father's original settlement. At the Highpoint itself. You can see it outlined against the sky, even in the dark. There's his old hut there. I haven't been up there for a few years, but I should be able get us there. It's defensible, I think, at least against the wildlife. That's a problem out here, at least at night in the open. Skut knows how to deal with it, I would think. It's quite a walk though."

"Take the other quad and the trailer," said Podge's father. He saw the look of doubt and said: "Mary—or Podge or Maddy, can drive it. We had one on Metheglin."

"You could go with them, Sir. I can go alone."

"Driven a quad before?"

"No, Sir," admitted Skut. "A tractor, yes."

"I'll take you. I owe you my family's safety. Mary, take my flechette…"

"You might need it," said Podge's mother. "We have Podge's one, and Sarah's shotgun." She kissed him. "Now, get on with it. Podge, go to the computer. To think I would ever say that!"

"Right," said Podge's father. "Podge. Look after your mum and the others…until I get back, son."

Skut saw his friend sniff and swallow. *Scared,* said Snarky.

Skut knew exactly how that felt.

SIXTEEN

The quad trip was mostly uneventful. They didn't go fast—it was too dark, and Snarky was able to alert them to two hunting creatures and a mass of patratti being chased along the wall. Skut was glad that Snarky's weird senses could find the gate in full darkness, and even tell them that there was no-one in the containment lab. The key-card got them through and Skut parted from Podge's father. "You could go now, Sir," he said, wishing he didn't feel he had to say it.

"I'll probably be safer in the lab here, than out there, sitting still," said Podge's father. "If you're in trouble, send your little dragon to fetch me. I'll see if I can find any useful stuff in here, while you're out. I brought a torch with me from the workshop."

So, Skut set out. He soon discovered that the Ghats were better organized by now. They had set up emergency lights along the road—admittedly, far apart, and not that bright, but lights. And he could see a number of vehicles driving around, with men and torches.

"Warn me, Snarky," he said quietly, taking a deep breath, and being glad that he'd sneaked out to get Snarky food, in the dark before, by this route. It wasn't that far to the apartment, but there was a party of soldiers with torches marching along the road. He ducked deep into the shadows— behind the bins just across from the place where the raised beds had been. There was a dim light in the apartment, and as soon as the soldiers had passed, the torch-light having flashed across the bins without shining on him, he ran to the back window, which was slightly ajar. He was about to call out, quietly, when he heard someone knock loudly at the front door of their one-room apartment. He ducked beneath the sill as torch-light speared above him. "Identify yourselves," snapped a voice in a slight accent.

"I am Nils Harkkson. This is my wife, Dr. Helga Harkkson, Sir," said his father.

"The list says there should be three residents here," said the accented voice.

"My son is not here," said his father, calmly. "We would like to find him. He was with his friends. Perhaps he stayed with them, being too scared to come home."

There was a meaty slap. "Sir, when you speak to an officer."

"Sir," said his father. "We are very worried about him."

"He'll probably turn up. Come, both of you. We'll send you up to the ship for further questioning. I don't like your tone. Yuvra, you march them up to the ship. And see you get back sharply."

Skut, horrified, heard the next door being knocked on,

and looking across to the road, his father and mother were being escorted by one of the men in their fish-net uniforms. He had to think, fast. They were being marched toward the containment lab on their way to the ship. He could get ahead, by nicking through several back gardens. There were some bushes at the roadside near the containment lab. He ran there, feeling the butt of his flechette pistol. Could he shoot a man? Would the man shoot his parents or him, before he died? He just didn't know. He could see them now, walking down the road, the Ghat soldier slouching behind. He only had to raise that rifle ten inches...

Father getting ready to attack

"You can talk to him?"

Can

"Tell him I will try and hit the guard's rifle," said Skut taking a careful bead.

I zap. When he comes past bush. Father says careful. Surprised.

The trio walked on. His parents had passed him now, where he was standing in the shadow. Then Snarky launched. The soldier caught the movement out of the corner of his eye, and then got 500 volts through the barrel of his rifle. His yowl was cut off by Skut's father hitting him on the chin—and his mother kicking his legs out from under him. His father dived on the rifle and Skut was pushing his flechette into the man's chest. "One sound and I'll shoot," he said, his voice squeaking slightly.

But the man didn't make one sound. His head just lolled forward. His mother made the sound instead. "Oh, my boy. We have been so worried."

"Me too, Mama. But can we go quickly to the containment lab? Podge's papa is waiting there."

His father had got to his feet by now, rifle at the ready. Then he looked at the soldier, and son, and in the dim light, Skut could see the flash of his father's teeth in his blond beard. "Mama, you take this rifle. Shoot anyone you see following us." He grabbed the soldier and tossed him over his shoulder. Years of farming made his papa very strong. "Shoot him if he tries anything or makes a noise, son. Let's go. We'll break out of the containment lab..."

"What's this?" asked his mother, looking at Snarky.

"I will tell you later mama. Let's just go, quickly."

"It looks like a storm-dragon," said his mother, "But they are supposed to be about six foot long."

"Snarky is a baby, mama. Now come quickly."

She did, but Skut got the feeling that if anyone had come up behind them, she would not have noticed, she was too busy looking at Snarky.

In the containment lab, there was another surprise. Podge's father had another prisoner, tied up.

"They came into the office, and started picking through stuff. They didn't expect me," he said. "I thought I might take this one along with us for questioning. They're worthless as hostages. We value life, Ghats don't. Or at least not the lives of foot-soldiers." He also had two more rifles. Skut didn't ask questions about what had happened to make it two rifles, and one prisoner. He just understood that Podge's dad was a lot more dangerous a man than he'd realized.

"We could take both, and ask questions separately," said papa. "But they may slow us down. And we have to break out of here. What about your family, Robert? Skut could go with his mama if we need to go and get them."

"Your boy got them out already. And we have a key-card that will get us out, and a quad and trailer outside."

Skut's mother asked: "Where did you get that storm-dragon son?"

"I found him at the first-tide tier, Mama. He was going to be killed."

"You can tell her all about it later, boy," said Podge's father. "Let's get out of here, first. There may be a problem out there. I dropped the other body there, and something came out of the dark and grabbed it. It made a noise like a lion with a gut-ache."

"Eliaz," said papa. "They like the smell of blood. They always sound fierce, but they are really scavengers. They only come out in full dark. And the first moon will be up soon."

They went out, cautiously, shining the torch, but there were no predators, as Snarky told him. Mr. Greene had some strong cable ties, so they tied up the second prisoner, and Skut and his father got to ride in the trailer with them, while Mama rode on the pillion. Skut—having ridden pillion on the way out—found out that it was a lot more comfortable than the trailer. In spite of that, Skut found he was really exhausted, and falling asleep, cuddling Snarky. He woke up, just at third moonrise, inside a rough-built hut, with Snarky telling him he was hungry. Well, at least that was familiar.

He sat up. "I'll feed you, but we must go and get Pru's grandfather."

"I had a try already," said Podge. "Sorry. You were passed out tired so I borrowed Snarky and we went down before first moonrise—me, my dad and yours. But when the Ghats couldn't get out, they shot out the lock on the gate. So now they have a squad on the gate, and they're guarding the power unit. We didn't have time to go in another way. Besides, they are probably guarding all the gates by now. Those two captives had belt-radios, so we're listening in. Dad knows enough of their language to follow pretty well."

"Where is everybody?" asked Skut.

"In the other hut. Well, your dad is out getting some meat. Pru said Snarky would need feeding, and your mother sent him off. Why did you hide Snarky from her? I mean, she's like a tiger guarding its baby."

"I didn't know," said Skut. "She's kind of fussy about her 'birds' too, I guess. She knew what he was, straight off. Seemed very excited about it." He stood up, stretched and yawned. "Is there any food? I am as hungry as Snarky. But I guess we weren't thinking about bringing anything."

"We were. Or at least my dad was. After Metheglin... well, we all had what he calls 'bug-out bags' packed. It was why we were so near the gate. It's not a lot, but we have dried rations."

PODGE HAD BEEN glad to be turned loose onto the Council's computer system, while in the workshop. He knew what he was doing there, he knew he was better at it than anyone else...certainly around here. He gave them a nightmare—the power went out twenty minutes later. And then after two hours, came back on. And then dropped one of its phases. And then blinked out completely for half an hour.

That was his 'happy' time. His miserable time was knowing what his dad meant. Knowing the Ghats and their cruelty and how brutal they could be. And knowing his father had just put responsibility on his shoulders. It meant his father knew he might not come back. He'd managed to largely wipe that from his thinking. Not his memory, never. He'd known and understood what risk dad was taking, fighting off the Ghat invasion on Metheglin. Others hadn't come back, or had been wounded worse than his dad.

And then his closest friend—friends, because you couldn't really think of Snarky as a pet—had gone off to take risks that Podge understood, and they didn't, without him. Part of him didn't expect them back, and he wasn't sure he knew how to deal with that. It was like a sore tooth of worry.

The ride through the dark to this place had been the same kind of thing. He knew, from Skut, that Skut thought of the uplands, away from the massive tides, as being as safe as houses...but it depended on the houses. There were still predators out here, even if it was nothing like below the tide-lines. The waiting in the huts had been awful, but not as bad as seeing Skut carried in by his father. He'd almost wanted to hit him, when he'd been told he was just asleep. The trip they had taken down to see if they could liberate Pru's grand-father was almost a relief. He was doing something, but he had two adults he could trust to make the decisions for him, and the others were safe. He'd gone through that brief bit of believing that they could do it all easily now...and then there'd been the guards at the gate. He did not want old Mr. Loper taken away as a slave. Actually, he didn't want anyone at all taken away.

He'd kept a look-out while the two prisoners were questioned, and then stripped to their underwear—revealing a small, two-shot hand-gun and two knives—as well as a few bits of jewelry, plainly loot. They used the quad to take them off to drop them into a strange hole walled with very sharp spikes, and with a little pool at the bottom.

"Won't they just climb out?" asked Podge

Skut's father had laughed grimly. "That's a Yin-yin nest or trap. The eggs are in between the spikes. The Yin-yin birds will come check on it soon—the traps emit a noise the Yin-yin can hear when they have prey. They'll close the top with more spikes and guard them. They keep live prey for their young. The eggs start to develop as soon they have prey in the trap. The prisoners have got three to four days before the little Yin-yin hatch and burrow into them. I cleared them out of our land. They normally catch spill-deer. Those men had better hope we're still alive to get them out."

Podge shuddered. "We could have driven into one of those in the dark."

"So you could. Vann's World is not for the unknowing or careless. But we'll teach you how to live on it. It is a good place, once you understand it."

That was his opinion, thought Podge. He had gone to rest after that, on the other bed in the hut where Skut was asleep, but he'd struggled to get to sleep, and had been glad when Skut woke.

Dawn was close, and they met Skut's father while on their way to the other hut in the compound. There were actually three buildings here but the other one was plainly a stable or animal shelter, that now had the two quads parked in it. They were all dug into the bank, roofed with turf, and walled with rock, with a sheltered path between them.

When they had driven up that night, Podge hadn't even seen the huts until Pru's mum had stopped and pushed aside the woven brush gate.

"Looks a bit like home," said Skut, sounding a little more cheerful.

"Oh. I didn't know. I thought you lived in a house like we have."

Skut's father was carrying three skinned and gutted Patratti. "No," he said. "This is like our home. Materials we have to bring in are expensive. Winter is cold. The wind and rain are hard. There are no large native trees outside the second-tier forest—and that's not real wood, just water-filled seaweed."

The other building had plainly been the main part of the Loper's old home. There was a big fireplace, and various wicker seats. Pru was asleep next to her mother on a day-bed next to the low window. It was pretty small as windows went, but it let in the moonlight. "Maybe an hour before dawn," said Skut's papa. "Any news on that radio, Robert?"

The answer was interrupted by Snarky—who had been sitting on Pru and was being studied by his mother, flying around Skut and fussing about him *SKUT! FOOD!*

Snarky plainly hadn't tried to 'speak' just to him, so not only did he wake the sleepers, but Skut's mother dropped the cup she was holding and stared really hard at Snarky and her son. She said "Skut! It spoke! The storm-dragon. It spoke!"

"Yes mama," said Skut. "He does, sort of. He's hungry."

"But he must have food!" she said, urgently.

Food. Meat. Patratti!

It was kind of hard to tell whether Skut's mother was

going to fall into her own mouth or not. But his father laughed, and handed one of the patratti to him. "Here Skut. Cut some off for him. Now Robert…"

"They've figured out that we're outside. And they plan to send a squad with one of their tracker lizards—the iguanons—out, at eight in morning. The commander wanted it now, but it's too cold for those lizards of theirs. They're the size of a Saint Bernard, and don't function when it is cold. But they can track anything. They were fetching clothes both from your apartment and our house for the scent. I don't know if they'll figure out that we used the quads. Those broad tyres don't leave much track, and they're city bred. They rely on the iguanon. We'll have to shoot it, or it will track us anywhere—and they're notoriously hard to kill."

"Papa," said Skut, thoughtfully, "What time is full low tide?"

"At six-fifty," said Skut's father.

"Remember how we used to lay scent-trails for the patratti? If we led the Ghats down below the tide…it comes in quite fast, and well, we know what to avoid, but would they?"

His father nodded. Turned to Podge's father. "How well can these things swim?"

"They're from a desert world. They might be able to swim, but it seems unlikely to me. Can we move across to something cut off by the tide?"

"It's possible. Tell me, does their home-world have moons? Do you know?"

"Definitely not."

"Right," said Skut's father. "I want your dirty socks please. All of you. And if it is all right, Robert, we will take one of the quads and a rifle. And those socks. They want to follow a scent trail, we will give them one. Skut, my boy?"

Skut, who had been cutting strips off the patratti and feeding them to Snarky, stood up. "Yes Papa."

"You are rested enough to come with me, son?"

Skut nodded, eagerly, and Snarky leaped to his shoulder.

"You can't take the storm-dragon into danger," said his mother. "I still have so much I have to find out about it. I had hoped to have one to study from before you were born, Skut. Oh. And you two also must be careful. But I know you will be."

Skut's father laughed and kissed her. "We'll take care. And you can study later. After we have dealt with these invaders."

SEVENTEEN

Skut was deeply happy, in an odd way. On the farm he had trailed his father everywhere, from the time he could remember. This felt like going back to the way things had been, then. He was a little sorry Podge couldn't be with them, but papa wanted to move fast, if they were to set a trail to the first tier and allow the iguanon to learn about how fast the tide could come in.

He soon realized that his father wasn't just giving them the tide, but making sure that the city-bred Ghats discovered the joys of the tidal forest and lower tide pools. Snarky had a job, too. He got to drag the socks—including Skut's own—though the scrubby bushes and down behind the ridge that led to a gully which led down to the next tide-line, where the second-tier forest was sagging flaccid. The tide was still slack, but it would turn at about seven. They moved cautiously through and down to the lowest tier, selecting pools to jump or skirt, making sure not to walk too close to the coralline spikes. They moved fast—faster than Skut would have dared to go on his own—but now he was a part of a team of three. They got back to the quad at dawn. It was parked just behind a low ridge and not visible from the settlement. Skut thought they would go back, but his father stopped part way up, and hid the quad behind some Withy-willows. "We'll keep watch from the ridge-line. If need be, we'll shoot and then run, and draw them off." He looked at the Ghat rifle and grimaced. "This will not be much good at long range...not even too accurate beyond 100 yards. Well, I suppose it was just a foot-soldier's weapon."

By now the sun was up and they lay on the grass just behind the ridge, hidden by a little rock outcrop, and looked at the settlement a couple of miles away. "I think we have about an hour," said his father. "Why don't you tell me about this little animal, eh? While we watch." So Skut told him, leaving nothing out, not even why he'd run away. Papa listened thoughtfully. He made very few comments, except to lead him on, and watched the gate. Eventually he said: "They come out. And the tide just begins to push, I see."

They could see the Ghats and the questing iguanon. "Looks like...twenty men, altogether. Ah. But two stay behind to guard the gate."

The cavalcade disappeared from view and then re-appeared on the broad lower tier, following their trail out toward the outer margins. The soldiers were spread out in a V behind the iguanon. Maybe that was clever in some places, thought Skut. But not on the tide-flats, between the coralline spikes and mushrooms. The men were not moving very fast, either.

"They are two down," said papa with satisfaction. "Injury, perhaps. Ah. There goes another." They could hear the distant sound of shots and see the V had broken into a semi-circle. They were plainly shooting into a pool. There would not be much to gain from that. The 'pools' too often connected with the sea, and the predators, like the slake-eel, would pull their prey under the coralline surface. The whole of the lower tier was basically a sponge-like network of tunnels and caves. After the soldiers spent some time, which they did not actually have to spare, the Ghat soldiers continued. Papa also noticed that one man returned to the gate. "His companion did not make it."

The iguanon continued to lead—they'd made sure to touch the scent to high places and the safe edge of the spikes. But they could see that the dry surface of the lower tier was beginning to turn into a sheet of water. Waves were now lapping over the edge of the tier, but it would also be coming up through the sponge of the coralline. Skut would never have been that close to the outer edge, and would have been making for the second tier as fast as he could safely go by now. There'd be shoals of little tide-eels and glass-fish skimming around their feet, taking the chance to feed on the protein rich foam and any damaged coralline polyps. Coralline pieces were broken off by the waves, the tide, and the bigger fish. The small fish would eat anything they could get their little mouths onto. They'd be biting tiny bits out of the soldiers' boots. The iguanon had plainly lost the scent, and the soldiers were milling about, maybe half a mile from the rise of the second tier, and by now the flats were awash with water with coralline spikes sticking up like teeth. It was horrible to watch, in a way. He knew, if they started walking as fast as they could, that they had a chance of reaching at least the second tier. That was still cross-able now. But every minute they delayed, the worse their situation got. The Ghats were slavers, invaders, murderers. But, knowing what he knew, he was still hoping they'd decide to run. Some would fall in holes, but to stay was to die.

Plainly they had no idea what a tide was, or what it meant here, because they wasted another couple of minutes milling about in confusion before starting to head back—but they were trying to go back the way they'd come, not heading straight for high ground. The water must be mid-calf now, and the iguanon suddenly started snapping and biting the water. Tark might be a tasty eating fish, but they were taking bites from the tracker lizard. It was thrashing about, and that was one thing that one really didn't do. It would call in bigger, nastier things.

The iguanon vanished in a welter of foam and splashing. The remaining Ghats climbed the razor-edged coralline spikes. A few more shots were fired. There were now eleven tiny, distant people, on a group of spikes.

Then they saw a troop carrier being driven through the glutinous second-tier vegetation and mud. It nearly got stuck, twice, but it managed in showers of mud and second-tier trees to splatter through to the first tier. The driver had plainly decided that hell-for-leather was the right answer, but he had to dodge between the spikes. Still, he got to within thirty yards of the stranded troops, when he hit a spike and slowed down. The weight of the troop carrier must have broken through the surface of the fragile coralline, and water surged up around its belly. Even from here they could hear the screaming of its engine as the driver tried to get it free.

"We can go now," said his father, grimly. "They are dead."

He was about to stand up when Skut grabbed his arm. "Radios, Papa. They might see us and tell others where we went even if they can't follow us."

"You are right. Besides, I don't think it will be long now. Look."

The commotion had attracted a fair of diving hamerkops and the water around the spikes was beginning to boil. The water would be at least two feet deep and thick with fish attracted to see if this meant something to eat. There was some desperate shooting going on, but the only thing that could have saved them—staying calm, and a shallow-draft boat—were not to be seen. What was seen was another troop carrier. This one, however, did not do as well—or as badly—as the first. This driver went cautiously, and straight down into the mud. It got stuck in the edge of the second-tier, barely a few yards in. They did fire their autocannon at the hamerkops and might even have hit a few, as the crew and another squad that rushed out the gate and with the next troop carrier, struggled to drag it free. They managed eventually, but they had to tow it back. As far as the squad who had been trapped out on the Coralline spikes...there was nothing to be seen, just water now, and the trees on the second-tier were beginning to swell and rise as water flooded around their roots.

"Time to go and join the others, son," said his father, tiredly. "I do not think they will venture onto the low tide-flat again."

Skut nodded. "It is strange to think I used to play out there, Papa."

"This is not their world, son. You have learned how to live here. Your friend...he will learn, but do you think he or my friend Robert could survive here without us?"

Skut thought about it. "If they stayed in the uplands...maybe."

"Ja," said his father. "So, if these Ghats come hunting us it will be in the uplands. They are not stupid either, and here we only have a few traps for them. If they have some kind of flier, we are in real trouble."

PODGE HAD HAD LESS time to worry about Skut than he'd thought. Skut's mother wanted to know all about Snarky—particularly about his ability to talk to them, but also about Snarky's ability to 'see' through walls, and to generate shocks.

"The reports we have about storm-dragon are that they hunt in groups. There have been several attempts to capture one." She pulled a face. "And two of the attempts ended in deaths. The third just failed to find any, although they had been seen in quite large numbers a mere day before. Now we know why. Oddly, the gillbies—the little flying animals I am working with—are electrosensitive. They catch their fish in murky water, and that means they do not have to rely on their eyes underwater. And there are Earth fish, the Knife-fish, one of the Gymnotids, which generate powerful electric shocks with biological batteries. One species that does this, *Electrophorus electricus*, the so-called electric eels, combine being able to deliver more than 800 volt shocks, with being able to sense their prey in murky water by detecting electric fields, AND they communicate to mates via some system of electro-transmission. It seems these storm-dragons are similar. Well! But it is this 'speech' I wish to get the bottom of."

Podge was deeply relieved to have Skut and his father back. Not only was he glad they were safe, but it meant that he could stop being questioned. Maddy's nose was really out of joint that she'd been the only one not to know, and she was just as fascinated, and as bad, about questioning him.

His father had been carefully listening on the radio to the Ghats communications. Just after eight he said abruptly, "The iguanon has picked up a trail. I hope it's the one they laid, not us going to the workshop. I brought a monocular from that lab. Mom has it for watch-keeping. It's time I relieved her anyway. We may have to flee this spot if they're coming this way. We should have made a plan on where to go."

They all went out to where Podge's mother was watching the settlement through a tiny slit window in the wall of the shed where the quads had been parked.

To Podge's relief she said: "They're heading out onto the tide-flat."

Skut's mother said, with a sort of scary finality: "Well, that is the end of them, then."

Podge's mother looked away from the monocular, and blinked. "But...isn't this just to lose the trail? Convince them that they can't follow us?"

"The tide tiers are very dangerous," said Pru's mother.

"The tide comes in faster than a man can walk. It's dangerous to run down there. And many of Vann's World's most dangerous creatures live and feed there. The tides bring them food. Smaller creatures try to stay shallower than where the very big can go."

"Three moons, Mama. It's a big three-body problem," said Podge.

She looked at him with narrowed eyes. "No wonder you didn't say much about this fishing. Still, surely the worst they'll do is get wet. I mean, they'll run once the water starts rising. It looks quite flat."

"I will be surprised if any get away," said Skut's mother.

His father, still listening to the radio, said: "Well, the first one has just been stung by something. They're sending him back with someone."

"The second-tier is more-or-less safe until the water gets there. That stage of the tide is big and fast."

Taking turns to watch through the monoculars, they saw how the tide dealt with the invaders.

EIGHTEEN

When Skut and his father got back they discovered that the others had followed the events, much as they had. There was food ready, and some security in knowing all the escapees had survived and were all together. Then Podge's father said: "Council of war time. We need to decide what to do. We probably can't remain here safely for too long. They might have had a lesson, down below the tide line, but they'll know—or work out—that we can't live down there. And someone may work out that this is a good lookout place."

"There are several rock stacks on the far side of Highpoint," said Pru's mum. "You can get across to them at low tide, but the rest of the time they're cut off."

"Might work in the short term, but from questioning those prisoners, their ship is too small for all the captives. They plan to negotiate a bigger ship to take the prisoners and hostages back, after they capture the VIP ship. That means they'll be here for a while. Ghats themselves may not know tides and the sea, but they can force charter captains into taking them by boat."

"We could steal a boat and be off to Faraway," said his mother. "But that leaves all the people here..."

"Father," said Podge. "What happens if the incoming ship gets warned?"

"I tried a while back," said his father. "I sent a message and photograph to Lieutenant-Colonel Morgan. I was absolutely right that there was trouble coming. I just don't understand how the GM was guiding Commander Ishmaeli around, and obviously co-operating with them, giving them safe passage past our missile shield."

"Well, I was thinking...you know when we came in, they had the planet and then the archipelago, then, like, the island on the viewscreens? Do you remember that show we saw back in the DP camp? The one about the castaways—and them writing 'HELP' on the beach-sand for the search planes?"

"Yes, but to be seen from space—even when they zoom in on the island?"

"I sort of have an idea. I mean, I saw three programmable mowers in the Workshop. Is there any paint? Like quite a lot?"

His father laughed. "There are five forty-four gallon drums of road-marking paint. Heaven knows why someone ordered so much. There is an electric pressure sprayer too. I suppose we could spray a pretty big sign, if we could get in there."

"I too was thinking that we might, well, help ourselves and help the people in the town," said Skut. "You see, I was thinking maybe tonight, when it was dark, Snarky and I might go and try and rescue Mr. Loper. Only...I think they will be guarding all the gates now and the street lights will be on. So, I thought maybe we could knock a hole in the wall. I mean, papa could with a tractor, I'm sure the front-end loader could do it easy. I thought...maybe if we made a whole lot of holes, they have to guard them to stop people escaping. And you said, Papa, there were only one hundred and eighty of them. They will be too busy guarding to chase us. Maybe people will get away, too."

"Maybe they get shot, but it is better than being a slave," said his father, approvingly. "It will be dangerous, driving the front-end loader. They will shoot at it. I will do that, and it will distract the guard while you get the mowers away, Ja."

"Well," said Podge. "When he was moving your garden...dad showed me the front-end loader has a laser level blade control. I mean, it adjusts the steering and the level of the bucket. If we can set that, we could start it going, and just jam the throttle, it could be set to drive along the wall and push it over. Nobody would have to be in it, after that."

"These boys," said papa, shaking his head, and grinning.

"How will we keep them out of jail?" said Podge's father, laughing. "Especially that one of mine."

"I am not going to let anyone put either of them in jail," Pru, who had been listening quietly informed them. "Maddy and I and Snarky will keep them safe."

Houses. Snarky informed them.

"He means safe as houses," Skut explained.

"He...appears extremely intelligent," said his mother. "That's conceptual, not just word recognition."

"You can study him later," said papa. "Now we just need

to work out how to get into that workshop for long enough, and then get out, without getting shot."

"Well, everyone else is coming up with clever ideas," said Maddy, "I think we should give them a ghost. You know, like the Haven spooks on Metheglin."

"They had projectors and smoke for that," objected Podge. "Made it look like monsters were flying at them."

"Well, you have him," she said, pointing at Snarky.

"You are not to risk him flying and being shot at!" protested his mother.

Brothers. Hunt together. Snarky informed them.

Of course, that got both the girls announcing they wanted him to be their brother too, and Maddy pointing out he'd be an improvement. It was funny. Maddy obviously thought that her big brother was the best...but would no more tell him so, than Podge would admit that he looked after her. "You have to eat raw fish together. Share your hunting."

There was a moment of silence, "Eugh. Okay," said Maddy.

"Not a very big piece, I hope," said Pru, warily.

"Huge and still wiggling," said Podge, with a wink to her that Maddy wasn't supposed to see.

"Ignore him, Pru. He's just being horrid. Brothers," said Maddy, disgustedly.

Brothers. Wriggling good.

"Huh. He's already just like a brother," said Maddy. "So, what do you think of my idea? Snarky could tow the ghost behind him like a kite."

"I think we can make something of it without putting the storm-dragon, or ourselves, in danger," said her father.

"I was thinking of harvesting stinger pods," said papa. "We could throw them."

"Or have Snarky drop them. If it's dark, he will be safe," said Podge.

"Well, Papa, what about skunk-fruit?" asked Skut, beginning to laugh. "We saw some, remember?" He had to explain that skunk-fruit kept anything from eating their seeds in a rather special way. The fruit, which got tossed from the second-tier tree when the tide came in, burst like bad eggs when they landed. The gluey goo that came out of them was so vile that even Vann's World's creatures wouldn't go near it, and so the tasty seeds could germinate safely.

"All good ideas," said Podge's father. "But for now, I think we need to take it in shifts to rest and keep watch. I've set up the other radio to charge off the quad, but listening in on this one it appears that a lot of their troops are sick."

"Good. That will give them less men to spare to come searching."

They still did come looking however, but not in force. It was early afternoon when Skut was awakened. "There are two squads of twenty moving up from the settlement. Looks like someone decided to look for us."

The two quads could move out without being seen, so they collected what they had, and headed to load them up. "We can't quite get across to the offshore rock-stacks yet," said Skut's father, worriedly.

"Hang on. There's chatter..." said Podge's father. "Er. One group seems to have run into some kind of wildlife they decided to shoot. They say it looks like a snake with a lot of legs, and a massive mouth"

"Crocopede. They're hard to kill and very bad-tempered

if disturbed. They haven't much brain, and a hide full of bony plates."

"They have called the other squad to come and help."

"They'd do better to run in different directions."

"I'm not telling them that."

"If they hadn't shot at it, it would have left them alone," said papa

"I'm not telling them that either! I think one of us should go back and watch with the monocular. We'll wait and be ready."

So Skut's father went. A few minutes later he came back. "We can go back. The survivors are retreating."

"Yes," said Podge's father. "They're saying that any people out here will be killed by the wildlife. The other troop got among some bushes that had some kind of animal which ripped off half of a man's leg, before they killed it. A big hairy horrible thing with a mouthful of teeth."

"A loor, probably. How many did the crocopede get?"

"Four. But there are a number of injured. They scattered and it chased down one man and the rest got away. But it is not dead. They don't want to go near the area again. In fact, they don't want to venture outside the walls again. They think this place is hell."

"Well, we'll see if we can give them some devils then," said Skut's father. "We will go and fetch some skunk-fruit and other little gifts for them."

"I've thought about a 'ghost' and my wife wants to make scarecrows to put in the front-end loader. Then they'll try to shoot those and not the machine."

A little later the ship took off from the landing field. "Have they left?" asked Podge, hopefully.

His father looked through the monocular. "Guards are still on the gate at Lopers. No, I think they've moved it, just so there is nothing to raise any suspicion when the Premier and his entourage arrive. Probably set down a reasonably long way off, rather than hang in orbit where they can't help but be seen."

They went on preparing.

By twilight they were ready. Nervous, but ready.

NINETEEN

H unting!
"They're not food, Snarky. And you're to be careful, see."

Scary good, Skut

That sort of summed up Snarky...and Skut, thought Podge. They kind of liked it scary. He...he still thought of his dog being shot. He didn't want Snarky shot. The storm-dragon fluttered off Skut's shoulder and landed on his, and nuzzled against his cheek. Well, Snarky knew what you felt.

They moved in single file, keeping out of sight, carrying the rough baskets carefully—they'd brought a quad as close as they dared, to spare Podge's father walking too far, but he had to walk the last hundred yards to the gully that ran parallel to the wall, where the trail had been set that had lured the men below the tide-line. Here Snarky took off with the first of the 'gifts' they'd prepared. They were in a small sea-grass basket, each of the three with a little parachute attached to a stinger pod. The first run worked perfectly.

The second did not. Either the parachute didn't open or it hit the side of the SMNR power station, and exploded. The sound and the stinger-darts provoked the guard to shoot into the dark, followed by a questing torch-light and yell of challenge. "I can shoot that guard," said his father, quietly. "The torch makes him a target. But then they would respond in force. There's at least two guards and we won't get both of them."

"How far can you throw?" whispered Skut's father.

It was too dark to see, but Podge was aware of his father flinging something, it hitting with a 'spulge' and him dropping into the ditch next to them.

The swearing from the guard was something special, even if Podge couldn't understand the words.

Drop more stingers?

"No. Go to the workshop," said Skut.

Even thirty yards away in the ditch, the wave of stench made Podge gag. What it must be like close up, he could hardly imagine. The guards did not have to imagine.

His father, listening in on the radio, showed a flash of teeth in the dark. "I never heard someone throw up on a radio before. They reckon they've killed something from Shaitan's own pit."

"And by the torch-light, they've moved back inside the gate," Skut informed them. "I bet they wish that they hadn't blown it down now."

"Let's move. They'll send an officer, and maybe more men." So, they crawled along the gully. Podge was glad Snarky had checked it for them.

"No one in the shed, Snarky?" Podge asked.

No.

From there it was a short distance to the building. Skut, as agreed, took up station at the door, watching as best he could for anyone coming out of the gate. Podge got onto programming the front-end loader, while their fathers got on with the heavy lifting and attaching the paint, more fuel, and three battery powered programmable mowers to the excavator. The mowers were quite big machines and too heavy to lift, but there was a roof winch. It squeaked, making everyone nervous.

Nasty. Gate

They stopped—Skut was using Snarky like a radio. There was a stirring of torch-light prodding the darkness. Voices. They didn't sound too happy, was all that Podge could say. But his father said, quietly: "That stink-bomb is working a treat. The officer just threw up too." They could still smell it from here.

They were able to get back to their work. Podge, having finished with the simple steering and level computer on the front-end loader—really it was very simple—went back to the power system and set the time for that to go out for a few minutes after the excavator was set to roll out. The ignition circuits had timers set in them—and then the keys were turned. "Three minutes, and all hell breaks loose."

Nasty. Gate.

They waited in nervous silence at the small walk-door, knowing that starting the diesel engines would surely call the guards, stench or no stench. Lights, again, questing into the darkness. The two fathers readied their rifles as a guard walked out...and bent forward to pick something up. In the torch-light they could see it was the parachute from one of the stinger-pods. They saw his companion raising his hand-held radio. And suddenly he screamed as sparks arced from Snarky, silhouetted above the man.

"SNARKY!" yelled Skut, leaping up, and drawing his flechette in one movement. The other guard dropped the parachute, to grab for his slung rifle.

Well, dropping the stinger pod was not wise. It naturally exploded, sending its needle tipped seeds spraying out. The guard staggered back, clutching at his eyes.

Fun hunt!

"Run! All of you!" snapped his father. So, they did, out into the darkness. Someone at the gate did fire wildly. Skut's father fired back. Then there was a diesel roar from the workshop shed. They ran on.

There was a shriek of metal as the front-end loader, full throttle, hit the shed double doors and burst out. That drew fire from the remaining guard, so he wasn't shooting or shining his torch into the dark, but at the front-end loader. A bullet screeched off the steel—possibly of the shed as the machine headed out of the light, turning toward the wall. To give the guard his due for courage—he ran after it. His father fired, and the torch went flying...just as the front-end loader hit the wall with a crash.

"Back off a bit more I think," panted his father.

They did. Within a minute his father said, "On the radio: Guard commander's trying to raise the guards. They have heard the noise."

As there was another splintering crash at this, Podge could quite understand why they were trying to raise the guard. He'd set the laser detector to make the bucket hit the wall at an angle. It ripped into the wall and then swung out to do it again, and again. Back in the dark they moved back towards the quad. Now it was all a matter of timing, and how long the front-end loader kept bashing into the wall, knocking panels out, before it stopped or was stopped.

The Ghats were quick to respond, and they were running out of the gate and after the front-end loader quite fast. But the front-end loader was also moving fast. The walls were relatively thin concrete sheeting with uprights. It wasn't slowing the machine much...but kicking stinger pods was slowing the followers. There was a lot of shooting going on—they seemed to be shooting at the 'driver'—which was a scarecrow of withy and clothes. With the throttle glued down, and the brakes and steering disconnected from the driver's controls, Podge's father wasn't sure how it could be stopped, unless the Ghats hit something essential in the engine. They'd done their best to strap some shielding onto that. The rubberized tracks would be near impossible to cut or break with rifle-shots. It would take luck to hit the hydraulic pipes.

"The commander is sending the troop carrier," said his father. "I wish like hell the excavator would get going."

At this it did, with a second diesel roar. The door was already smashed, so it just trundled straight into the dark. It caused more panic than a 'stopping it' reaction, to Podge's relief. The Ghat soldiers obviously thought it was going to attack from the rear, and it trundling off into the darkness appeared more of a relief than a cause to follow it.

"No saying what the troop carrier might do. It'll be faster than the excavator."

Fortunately, it seemed that the troop carrier was instructed to stop the destruction by the front-end loader, so it raced straight on along the torn wall.

Skunk-fruit, said Snarky, and grabbed the basket that the fruit was in and flew off after the lights of the troop carrier, while Skut tried to call him back. They could see the front-end loader in its light. The troop carrier fired...and managed, somehow, to miss. The shot merely added to the demolition of the wall. And then the carrier swerved wildly and hit the wall. Men spilled out of the back of it. It was too dark to see what they were doing, but they weren't firing.

Hole on top. Skunk-fruit in. Snarky informed them.

There was a moment of silence. Then Podge's father said, "In through the command hatch. In a confined space... Well, I think we can leave after the excavator now, Podge. Good luck, Nils and you too, Skut. You and that mad creature of yours."

Good?

"Very good! Good hunting!"

Not good hunting. Skunk-fruit spoils meat.

"Fun then," Skut granted. "Now we better do the rest, Papa."

Podge felt his heart, so elated a moment ago, fall again. Skut and his father were going in to try and get old Mr. Loper. Skut...well, he'd promised Pru. And Skut's father... well, he had said that there was a debt. And one thing Podge had realized about Skut's father: he'd pay his debts, no matter if the all Ghats in the world stood in his way.

"Yes," said Skut's father. "I think we can go in through one of the new holes."

Skut, in the act of standing up, said "Hush!"

Podge couldn't hear anything. But he knew from plenty of experience in detention that Skut could hear the tiniest noises.

"There is a vehicle. At the gate, I think. Electric, not much noise. I hear something squeaking and bouncing."

"Ja," said his father. "I hear. Coming closer. No lights though."

"They're after us. Must have night-vision gear," said his father.

"Snarky could..."

"He'll show up on infrared."

"It doesn't sound like a very big vehicle. And it's not moving very fast," said Skut.

"I'll see if there is any chatter on the radio," said Podge's father. He had it turned down very low, and put a cloth pad around it, so Podge could barely hear it, even right next to him.

"No," he said, quietly. "They're yelling at the troop carrier driver. And at the men to chase the front-end loader. Maybe it's an escapee."

"It's going a bit closer to the sea than we are," said Skut's father, plainly listening intently.

Snarky look

He came back a very little later. *Papa Papa Pru!*

"What! Did you tell him it was us?" said Skut.

I say Skut. Near. Nearly fall off machine. That made them all laugh.

"Let's take the quad to him," said Podge's father, sounding relieved. "I should have guessed. He's a tough old bird."

Not bird. Snarky informed them. *Chewy, could be.*

They were still laughing when they caught up with Mr. Loper, on his big-wheeled forklift trundling steadily along into the dark. Podge remembered he'd explained the outsize wheel as necessary for fetching goods from the farmers' boats. Well, the wheels also meant it had so far avoided getting bogged down. His first question on being greeted was: "My daughter and granddaughter, are they with you?"

"Up in your old huts on the top of the hill," Skut informed him. "They're fine."

"Well, that's a weight off my mind," he said. "Mind you, when they questioned me about you, boy, I guessed they might be with you."

Papa Papa Pru. Not right! Help

Podge and Skut, more used to Snarky's *speech* were first to react, jumping out of the slow-moving quad's trailer and running to the forklift, which was just coming to a stop. Between them they managed to stop Mr. Loper falling hard onto the ground, by falling with him instead. Skut's father and his were there moments later.

"Is he dead?" asked Skut, his voice rising.

"He still has a pulse," said Podge's father. "Let's have a little light, please."

Someone produced a torch and they could see his face was bruised, and one eye swollen shut. He was breathing, though. "That hand's a mess," said Podge's father. "Come on. Let's get him into the trailer."

"Ouch," said the old man, as they lifted him.

Podge never knew that a word could sound so good.

"What hurts?"

"My back. They beat me. And my ribs. Got a few kicks."

"If we get you onto the quad-seat behind Nils, do you think you could hold onto him? Be less bouncy than the trailer."

"Reckon."

"Right, if we chase the excavator, I will take control of that, and you can take him to the old homestead."

So that was what they did, and a few minutes later they were able to support him into the hut where the others were waiting, nervously. Pru's delight at seeing her grandfather was replaced by the shock of seeing his face, pale, bruised and cut. "Grandpop!" she shrieked running to him. "Are you all right?"

"A bit sore, my love. But I'll be fine," he said, patting her, as she clung to him.

Pru did not seem much consoled, but burst into tears. Snarky landed on her shoulders, put his tail around her neck and informed them *Papa Papa Pru chewy!*

That was strange enough to distract her, while the boys explained, and Mr. Loper was led to a chair—which he said he preferred, right then, to a bed, and examined by Mrs. Greene—very much in nursing sister mode. His back, when they stripped off his shirt—which was stuck to it with blood —showed bleeding welts and bruises. Two of his fingers, which she carefully strapped, were probably broken.

"Well, first they beat me up because you were missing," he said. "And then some of them came back to loot and steal, and tortured me to show them where the money was hidden. But I got my own back on them," he said. "A lot of them are very sick still. I knew they'd steal the alcohol, so I put laxative in all of it."

"I thought Ghat's were forbidden alcohol..." said his daughter.

"They might be. But it's never stopped looting soldiers. And it means they can't tell their officers why they're so sick."

"Oh, Pop! I am so sorry we left you there. If we'd stayed..."

"If you'd stayed they would have tortured you instead. I was never more grateful in my life. They're not killing people, or not many, but the Ghat soldiers are looting and beating people up."

"Well, I hope lots of people escape now. The settlement isn't a prison anymore," said Podge.

"I hope so too," said his father. "You were quick off the mark, Sir. I hope the rest are."

"Oh, I saw the gate-video from the office," said the old man. "And I had everything ready. As soon as they were busy I lifted a few panels out with the forks and drove out. I could smell what you lot were up to. That'll serve them right."

"Still, we've made a problem for ourselves. We may have a lot of people wandering around in the dark, unarmed, without food or water. Some of them know what they are doing out here. Most of them don't. We've tried to stop their target landing. We could be stuck here with a lot of people that we're trying to look after. The Ghats still have a lot of armed men, and a lot of hostages. After tomorrow we have a problem," said his father.

"But that is after tomorrow's problem," said Skut.

"Not really," said his father. "We'd better go look for escapees tonight and try and see if we can get them away."

"Well, they don't have to be unarmed, boys," said old Mr. Loper. "My forklift has a case of Flechette pistols I had for selling to the farmers and a case of ammunition and couple of my rifles. I hid them under the soap, detergent, shampoo and ladies' hygiene products before the looters arrived. They were looking for food and items of small saleable value, not those."

"Well, they can go on looking for it," said Pru's mother. "You're going to rest, Pop. When did you last eat or drink anything?"

"It's been a while," he admitted.

Podge and Skut, standing next to each other, found themselves being hugged by Pru. She still had Snarky snuggled around her neck. "Thank you for bringing my grandpop back!"

"He was doing a pretty good job of bringing himself back," said Skut, awkwardly.

"Snarky said he fell on top of you," she informed them.

"That was mostly Podge, and he doesn't squash easily. But Snarky's right. He's chewy. You take care of him, all right," said Skut.

She nodded, earnestly. "I want to pay them back for what they did to him. But I must get him better first."

TWENTY

S kut thought that if he had to have a little sister, one like
Pru would be OK, but having seen her lose her temper,
maybe even the Ghats might want to move off. He sort of
wondered what had happened to all the kids from school.
Wondered how the mean girls were liking this. And then his
thoughts turned to the three who'd come and sat at their
table, and he didn't feel so good.

Podge's father had come in by now, having parked the
excavator behind the ridge some distance off. The tracks
would be easy enough to follow, and they would have to
abandon this place anyway, come morning.

They left Pru and her mother to fuss over the old man.
Maddy was on guard duty with Skut's mama. The first moon
was up, but it was a night of scudding clouds so they had
moments of a relatively good view, followed by pitchy darkness, where there was not even starlight. The settlement was
still in darkness, but they could see the glow of what must

the emergency lighting here and there. "As good a time for fleeing the settlement as any," his father said.

"Let's check for chatter on their radios," said Podge's father.

There was certainly a cackle of that.

"Well," said Podge's father, after a while: "That's war for you. They never do quite what you expect. They're going door-to-door, and pushing all the people down to the Ocean View Hotel lobby. They'll keep them under guard there."

"They'll be packed in like sardines," said his father. "They will keep some, surely, to make the landing port look normal? They want the VIPs to get out of their ship, otherwise it may all fall apart for them, Ja?"

"I assume they'll pick a few people to make it all look normal," said Podge's father, frowning. "I imagine they'll keep family members—children, wives, husbands—as hostages to their behaviour. I think they'd planned to have an air of business as usual...let the most important people be loaded onto the hotel busses and the Mayor and the GM's vehicles. Now they must hope enough disembark before they try and take them."

"That means they'll be looking for us to disturb the landing, most likely. Well, we'll see if we spot any escapees. We're higher up and know what we're looking for. Unfortunately, the quad's batteries are quite low, and we'll want them for the run down to the sea-stacks. With this leg, I'm not that good at long walks, let alone running. Podge and Skut will just have to get on with the sign you planned, my boy."

"Dad," said Podge. "Could you help with the excavator? And getting the mowers down, maybe?"

"You help your boy, Robert," said papa. "We'll look for escapees, and lead them away. We have a few hours before dawn. We'll head for the fork-lift. It's not fast, but we can use it to carry things, and recover the flechettes and ammunition."

Skut, with Snarky on his shoulder, and his father walked a long way that night. There were two problems: one was that they had no idea if anyone had escaped, or where they would be. The second was they really hadn't made a plan of what to do with them, if and when they found them. It was probably just as well, Skut thought, that they did not find too many people, and mostly ones that really didn't need that much help. The first was a farmer who had got work at one the hotels, and he was already armed and capable of shepherding his family along. Other than pointing him at the idea of hiding out on one of the sea-stacks, and giving him another mag of flechette ammunition, he was easy. The next two were both skippers of charter boats and their families. They knew papa, and were grateful for a couple of pistols. They at least had some idea of what to look out for, particularly along the coast.

Skut was pleased to see Kate and Anne—two of the three who had come to sit at their table that last recess, it seemed so long ago—were part of this party, along with two younger children. "Skut! They were searching for you!" exclaimed Kate.

"Ja," said his father. "If not for my boy," he said with pride, "we would all of us still be captives. Now we fight back."

"I'm with you," said Kate's father. "Those scum have killed a couple of people, have beaten up a lot. Robbed us.

Tore my wife's necklace off her throat. The GM promised if everyone behaved we'd be fine. I thought...well, that's when the crashing started, and the ones that had been threatening to torture my kids if I didn't give them money ran off to see what was happening. I said to Sally, we get the kids, get Jimmy and the family, and see if we can get out," he jerked a thumb at the skipper. "And he thought the same thing, because from his place he could see that the wall was down. Then the lights went out, and the Ghats were running around like chickens with their heads cut off to deal with whatever was knocking pieces of the wall down. We just waited until we had a chance and got out of one of the holes and headed away. I'm not sure where we go now?"

Skut's father scratched his head. "You should pick one of the little islands you can walk to at low water. They are scared of the tide. But they may use the boats."

"Well, I wouldn't want to take a boat in there without a good skipper. Not someone like Norm," said his friend, poking him in the ribs. "That lot of sand-rats would be drowned before they got out of the bay."

"They will take a good skipper. Hold his wife or child with a knife to their throat. What would you do?" said Skut's father. "Look. Go on up the hill. When you reach near the top, sing out. Our wives and the girls, and old man Loper are there. They are going to the sea-stacks on the north around dawn. There are a lot of them and it is shallow, so not easy to bring a boat in. There are some caves in the rocks. We'll get everyone as safe as we can, and then see what we can do next."

This was more or less the pattern they followed with the rest of the people that they found—there weren't many. Of the nearly thousand people in the settlement, around fifty had seized the opportunity to flee. And almost all of those had some experience of life outside the walls of the settlement. There were a handful of exceptions, two young women who had been hotel staff, and one of the nurses and her young son of about five.

These they walked up the hill, to find Podge and his father also trudging up the hill. Podge had shared the paint with his clothes. "Chirp on the radio is that they are trying to clean up the mess the front-end loader made, dad says. And they're struggling with their troop carrier. They're trying to get things cleaned up before the VIP ship lands, at eight. They're a bit too busy to think of us, dad thinks."

"How did the sign-painting get on?" asked Skut.

Podge laughed. "It wasn't as easy as I thought. But there's a sign that says: "GHATS HEL"

"HEL?" asked Skut.

"We ran out of paint. Now we're going to take quad down. Dad thinks we can wire up the mower batteries to the quads. Give them a bit of a lift. And move the excavator. There's the fire we want to start too. A big smoky fire might get noticed. Dad says that the VIP's are bound to have a security detail going ahead of it."

Up at the old homestead everyone was preparing to leave. Skut concentrated on getting food for Snarky and left them to talk. But he drew the line when he heard that Podge and his father were going to set the excavator heading for the space-port with a fuel bomb and then flee to hide before they could cross over to the sea stack, as the tide would be in. His own father was also not going with them. He was to use one of Mr. Loper's rifles to attempt a long shot at the landing ship, just to try and frighten them. "The tide will be starting to go down by then, Papa, but the second-tier will still be flooded. Podge and his father will maybe have to hide in it. I can help them do that."

"I will, son."

He took a deep breath. "Papa. They will be shooting back." He couldn't quite bring himself to say 'if you are killed or wounded', but went on. "I need to be there, Papa. Especially...especially if you...can't. If..."

His father smiled. "Do you think I don't worry the same about you? And about looking after your Mama? But, ja, son. Two of us will make the second-tier forest easier. It's a good rifle, and a good scope. We have chosen a reasonable valley to escape down."

His mother made some more fuss, but in the end Skut went along with his father, Podge and his father, and one of the charter-boat skippers. "I used to do some serious competition shooting, and long-range scope correction," the skipper informed them. "Jimmy will just have to look after two families for a while. Do him good."

Before it was dawn, they were all in position. Podge and his father were due to join them after working on the excavator, getting it lined up and ready to trundle towards the settlement. The waiting was the worst bit—well, it would have been worse, except Snarky decided it was a good time to play ball. He actually managed to get Skut laughing before Podge joined him, the two of them about fifty yards off where the two men who were going to try and shoot at the incoming craft, to stop them opening their hatches. At exactly twelve minutes to eight—the time they worked out it would take the excavator to get to the landing field—Podge's father started the excavator, put the throttle on full and jumped out. He came running as fast as he could. It was only when he ran that you realised how badly his leg affected him.

And that was the last time that anything went to plan.

TWENTY-ONE

The excavator, big and orange, trundled down the hill. It hadn't done more than two of its twelve minutes before it came under fire, from several heavy weapons at the settlement. The excavator was still a great deal closer to them than was comfortable, great gouts of earth and explosions erupting around it, and then hitting it. It must have broken a track, because it swivelled towards them and one of the hydraulic lines on the boom must have burst. It sent a burning jet up into the sky before the fuel drums exploded. It was a fiery wreck—and then the gunners must have decided that they were hiding behind that ridge—or the ridge behind.

Earth showered them as shells exploded. Shrapnel screamed overhead.

And then abruptly the terror of it...stopped. They were all huddled down as flat as possible, and they had wriggled back from the ridge, but Skut risked a quick look for his father...he saw they had stayed in their position, but that a ship was descending. Early! Thank heavens.

If the ship had seen the sign, or even the smoky burning wreckage, it did not attempt to stop its descent. Skut didn't even know if they could. The ship drifted lower, into the trap.

Then when it could not be more than a hundred feet off the landing field, fire lanced out from it at targets in the settlement. Before the smoke of that could clear, several landing craft shot out from a hatch.

"The cavalry have come!" said Podge's father, as jump-troops spilled out of the landing craft, to the left and right of the settlement.

In a cloud of smoke, the ship set down.

"Well, that is the end of our problems," said the charter-boat skipper.

"No," said papa. "They put men into the second-tier forest. It will hurt or kill them. I will have to go down to them."

"They'll probably shoot you, Nils," said the skipper

"Ja," said his father with a shrug.

Fortunately, that was taken out of their hands by one of the landing craft swooping down towards them. "Put down the guns. Stand up and wave both hand in the air," said Podge's father. "We don't want to be killed because they take us for Ghats."

But it seemed there was no such danger. The landing craft dropped to a hover in behind the ridge. A door opened, and a ladder folded out. An armoured man in the doorway said: "The CO wants you. Jump to it."

So, they did. The pilot zipped fast and low to behind the now-landed ship and put them down to face a small, dapper man in combat fatigues and an armoured vest. He looked at them. "Wild Robert. I could have guessed. You seem to have stepped it up since Metheglin."

"Lieutenant-Colonel Morgan!"

"For some obscure reason they've made me a Colonel, Greene. I'll be with you in a few minutes. We have some issues on the flanks"

"I think you better talk to Mr. Harkkson, Sir. Now." The officer looked startled. "Your flanks are in danger," he explained.

The man's eyes narrowed. "Talk."

"It is very dangerous in the forest, Sir," said Skut's father. "I can guide them."

"My men are dangerous, and well trained," said the officer.

"The forest killed eighteen Ghats, yesterday, Sir," said Podge's father. "We didn't have to lift a finger."

"I still wouldn't be sure I had to take you seriously, if it wasn't that I've just had a report that one of my men is caught up in something like a tree with tentacles, that they can't get him free of, and they have been attacked by several creatures with big teeth," admitted the Colonel. "Shooting it doesn't have any effect."

"Better tell them I am coming, Sir," said papa. "And if you will send someone with my son to the other side, he can guide them."

"Well, thank you," said the officer. "But we'll just fly a carrier in to them if it's that bad,"

Skut's father shook his head. "You cannot land there. Not at this tide."

The officer looked at Podge's father, who nodded: "Local knowledge, Sir. Trust him. Remember Sindar Gorge on Metheglin."

"Yes. I do. Sergeant, get an escort for these two. Contact the flank points and tell them to stay put until they get their guides."

So, Skut found himself with two jump-troops for an escort, being taken to the second-tier forest. The tide had already started to retreat, but the trees were still full. "Please step exactly where I step," he said, hoping they would listen. "Some of the trees can be aggressive. And don't step in any pools. Ever."

They walked in the shadowy forest. He knew from their map the soldiers were only about a hundred yards in, but that could be a long way in the forest.

Snapper

It helped to have Snarky there to spot nasties, thought Skut, as he shot it.

"Sonny. Next time warn us!" said the sergeant,

"If I have time, Sir. There are not a lot of those. It's the tentacle trees that you have to watch for. You're getting too close to that one. Stick to where I walk."

"RIGHT," said Colonel Morgan, once Skut and his father had embarked on one of troop carriers. "Greene. Why don't you tell me what you can? The warning that Elharad Ishmaeli was scouting this place obviously got to us in time.

On the same day HQ got the request for a security detail for the Premier, as it happens. We put two and two together, followed up on the ship he'd come in on, and I got reconnaissance-in-force authorised. We had a stealth-scout orbiting from last night. You've been busy...as usual."

Podge's father laughed. "I had help. So, all our sign-writing was in vain, was it?"

"We thought it was some form of trap, at first," said the Colonel. "Nearly dropped a missile on it. 'Hel' seems appropriate though. And your efforts did show us exactly where their heavier weapons were emplaced, so we could neutralize them. Now, tell me what you can."

"There are about 160 of them."

"Before or after the eighteen?" asked the officer with just the hint of a smile.

"After. A few others have, well, met with accidents. Anyway, they've herded most of the citizens into the hotel lobby after we broke the wall. There'll be a few left in the town to make it appear normal. As you guessed, it was all to take high value prisoners."

"And how many hostages?"

"I'm guessing, Sir. Maybe 920? Possibly 950 at the most. They seem to have secured the co-operation of the settlement's General Manager at least."

"A tricky situation," said the Colonel. He sighed. "Well, government hostage negotiators will be here in three days. They'll take the situation from where we're at, then."

That was...dispiriting. Yes, they would try and get the hostages back. They were prepared to give the Ghats a great deal for that—which was why the Ghats persisted. On the other hand, they wanted their people freed.

SKUT, in the meantime, was very near to the hostages—or at least some of them. He had led the twenty jump troops through the edge of the forest. When he'd got to them, they'd only had an encounter with stinger pod tree, which their armour had saved them from the worst of, and having to haul one member of the squad out of a pool full of tentacles. The sergeant had given them a few words about following Skut—and putting their feet exactly where he put his. Skut led them to the ramp that led to the lower jetty, where they had gone fishing. The gate was locked. "Pity blowing it will make a noise. But it can't be helped," said the sergeant.

"Um, can we get hold of Podge...the other people who were talking to your...Colonel-whatsit?" asked Skut, "He can give me the code."

The sergeant grinned. "Colonel Morgan. And none of you boys heard that."

But he called through to their comms, and a few minutes later they were on the lower tier of jetties, under the broader high-water jetty above. The tide was still quite full so Skut warned them to stay back from the water. "The fish here will jump..."

"Sounds good!" said one of the troops.

"No Sir. Some are as big as you are. But they are all hungry. They killed all the Ghats that got into the water, and that was before the big ones even reached them," explained Skut.

Snarky winged off his shoulder and dived into the water at the edge, and came out with a wriggling tide-hopper. He dropped it at Skut's feet and took off again, and flew slowly along the roof.

Skut picked the fish up, and showed them the teeth—and cut it in strips for Snarky.

"The kid knows his stuff," said one of the troopers, approvingly.

People on top. School.

Skut said to the sergeant, quietly: "Sir, the hostages are above us, on the jetty."

"Any way we can get to them? Any guards? How do you know?" asked the sergeant, just as quietly.

Skut pointed. "Snarky can tell. And...if you listen really hard you can hear them."

"I'll take your word for it, boy. Let me get onto comms."

He did. "Your father will be bringing another three squads in. Apparently, the Ghats in the town folded, and either surrendered or got killed. Very few casualties. They really weren't expecting us, so it's just the ones with the hostages in the hotel. CO reckons they are using the kids as human shields to stop us from landing on the jetties and storming the place. They can shoot the kids from cover if we even try."

Skut looked at the water beyond the jump-trooper's shoulder. It was patterned with raindrops. "I've got an idea, Sir. Can you ask my father to bring Podge down? Up that ramp over there is the boat shed. I think there's a way through to the hotel...for the caterers. And there's a computer terminal. I know, Papa said the skippers do their bookings through it. You get Podge onto it. He's a wiz with anything like that. He can unlock doors, turn off lights maybe? And he can unlock the stairwell. Well, the code he gave us might work."

"I'll pass that on. Lights won't help much alas."

"Oh, they will, Sir. You see, it is going to rain. It rains pretty hard here, in the summer storms. It even chases the fish away. They don't like all the fresh water."

The man looked doubtful. "You'll see, Sir," said Skut. He knew you couldn't really explain it.

TWENTY-TWO

P odge, standing with his father, heard about this. His father turned to him and the Colonel: "If my son is going anywhere with young Skut, I'm going along. I know those two!"

"Says Wild Robert," said the Colonel, with a wry smile. "Well, can your boy hack into their computer system? Why am I asking? Of course, he can. And it's going to rain, is it? Might be good, the Ghat's are less likely to be used to it."

"Nobody is used to this place's summer rain," said his father. "I just hope the troop carrier gets back with the two hotel staff girls before it starts. They won't fly in this rain."

"That bad?" asked the Colonel.

"The record I saw is fourteen inches in twenty-four hours. Winter is windier, wild as can be, but the storms come and go. In summer, the winds aren't that bad, but it rains harder, for longer."

"I see. Well, it could still open opportunities. As soon as we can get a carrier here you'd better go and join the men under the jetties. I'll be in touch via the radio. With the hostage situation, we'll probably have to wait for negotiators."

"I'll have to switch the power on first, Dad."

His father chuckled. "Of course. Would the terminal in my office do or do you have to go to the workshop?"

"The workshop," admitted Podge.

So, it was in already sousing rain that Podge and his father, and a lot more troops, were escorted to join Skut on the lower piers.

Only... Skut wasn't there.

"Short of shooting him I couldn't stop him," said the sergeant, helplessly. "He waited until we were setting up at the stairwell...and then he untied a rope that hung down from the upper layer, so it swung out with him over the water. He went up it like a rat up a drain-pipe. I tried to get him to come down. He said he couldn't, he'd fall in the water and the fish would kill him. He said up there he'd just be another kid, and could tell us what was going on. He said... Podge would be able to talk to him."

Podge. Skut say he's fine. One guard, up against the doors. Trying to stay dry. Crawf here.

"He's fine. He says one guard, against the doors, trying to stay dry."

Lock doors hotel to Jetty. Open door down.

"Okay," said Podge. "Be careful, Skut."

Fun. Snarky told him.

Podge didn't transmit that part on to his or Skut's father.

"That kid...I don't know whether I want to whale him or shake his hand," said the sergeant.

"He is my son," said Skut's papa. "No one will punish him but me or his mama. And we will not tell her about it."

"All I can say is I wish he were my kid," said the sergeant.

"Can we get into the boat-shed?" said Podge. "Skut says it is wet and miserable up top and can we get on."

"How do you know?" asked the sergeant.

"It's a long story, Sergeant," said his father, "And one for telling once that job is done. Come on."

IT HAD SEEMED like a good idea to Skut, when he'd seen the rope. A good idea...until it swung out over the water and he had to climb it or slide down and fall off. And the higher up the rope he got the wetter and more slippery it got. It was not nearly as easy as he'd thought. The rain was coming down hard by then, which made it look even further because he couldn't even see the water thirty feet below. At least it probably meant they couldn't see much from the windows of the hotel. By the time he reached the slab of the jetty, he was exhausted and he had to reach over it to pull himself up. And he was out of pull. Straining, he looked up into the face of the kid huddling by the bollard. It would be the guy he'd punched on the nose, part of his mind thought. "Pull me!" he gasped.

And, wonder of wonder, the kid did. He looked numb and terrified, but he did it. Skut huddled gratefully on the pier, panting. The kid kneeled next to him, rain streaming down his big face. "Where did you come from?"

Fred wasn't the sharpest pencil in the box, thought Skut. "Come to rescue you."

The wild hope on the kid's mug, and his opening mouth made Skut put his hand in front of it. "Shh. You'll give it away." He sat up. The rain was like a solid wall of water now, sneaking into his parka collar. He felt like he should be steaming, he was so hot, but he knew it would get cold soon. He could see people huddled along the jetty surface, and crowding more densely toward the building.

Crawf Snarky informed him.

That was a relief. "Just stay calm, Fred. There are jump-troops coming, we'll get you out. Now I need to find Mr. Crawford."

The kid looked at Skut with a mixture of terror and hope. "He's out a bit further. Trying to make a shelter for the littles. Where have you been? They were searching for you."

"Outside. Fighting back. Take me to Crawf. And don't make a fuss or noise, or we won't get away."

They made their way to where Mr. Crawford was attempting to get the bigger kids to form a human shelter for the little ones. He tugged at the man's sleeve. "Sir."

"Not now..." and then he turned: "Harkkson! Where did you come from?"

"Come to organise a rescue, sir. I'll need your help. And," he said fiercely to the grade tens Crawf had been organizing, "you lot to shut up, or we'll be caught. I need to find out some things, Sir. Please come and talk to me. I need to know things like...how many guards are here now?"

He got all the details before Snarky told him Podge was below. All the children had been put onto the jetty in front of the hotel the Ghats had taken over—everyone, even mothers with nursing babies. Those were against the hotel windows, under the little bit of shelter the building offered. When the rain had started they'd begged to be let in, but the Ghats had refused. They'd only left one guard—obviously at the bottom of the pecking order—outside, warning them they could still shoot them through the glass.

"Sir," said Skut. "There's a trap door and a stairwell at the outside end of the jetty. Podge says they have it open. But his father says you must lead small groups down, otherwise there will be a stampede and people will fall over the edge."

The master nodded. "Can you take those youngsters down? The grade three's are in that huddle."

Crawf, when it came to giving orders, was pretty good at it. He had the grade ten kids he'd been using to shelter the little ones, walking slowly back toward the hotel to get the others to start edging out. Skut, by Crawf's instructions, had kids holding hands with each other, and then with him, and then he led them to the stairwell. The sergeant and five other jump-troopers were already up and hidden as well as possible—next to bollards and a fire hose and the navigation-light at the end of the jetty. There was not much cover, but in this rain no one could see very far. The sky was just chucking it down.

The kids he handed over to his father, who was waiting just inside the stair—and hopefully was less scary than jump-troopers. Skut smiled at his papa and said 'more' and walked back. In the next ten minutes they quietly ferried almost everyone away. Amazingly, just the women and little children huddled from the rain against the windows were left.

The sergeant called him in to the stairwell. "I'll crawl closer and might be able to shoot the Ghat, son. But for all that they say its storm-proof glass...the bullet might penetrate, and frankly, it is hard to see well enough to get a clear shot. Might be best to rush him."

"No," said Podge's father. "I'll deal with him. There were one or two adult civilians up here. The teachers, keeping the kids in order. I'll just be another one of them to the Ghat."

"I can't let you do that Sir...this crazy boy has already..."

"Colonel Morgan re-instated my rank from Metheglin, Sergeant. I'm Captain Greene of the Metheglin Irregulars. Wild Robert Greene. You may have heard of me," said Podge's father, in a voice that even made Skut start back.

But Skut said calmly, "I can get right close to him, Sir. And Snarky can shock him. You and Papa can help to lead them all away. Podge says he will set off the fire sprinklers in the front lobby to cause a distraction."

"Too dangerous."

"I'll just go and tell the women to get ready, not to panic and run, Sir. I'm just a kid," said Skut, not mentioning that Crawf had been organizing just that.

"Right. Then come straight back here. Your father and I will drift closer, and then, once you're back, we move in."

"Sergeant, you'll move backing teams along the edges of the jetty," Captain Greene decided.

Skut didn't wait to hear more, he was already walking through the rain. Snarky, who had mostly stayed dry burrowed away in Skut's shirt, pulled his buttons open and waited, ready at his waist.

Skut had his plans—but Snarky had his, too. The Ghat soldier wasn't looking, just huddling back against the doors, but he had a row of women standing in front of him to stop the rain blowing back in. Snarky flew along their legs—and then up to the broad lintel above the door. *Podge sprinklers. Wet.*

The last was probably about the rain. He dropped down and discharged his tail into the fellow's neck. Podge's father was already running in and grabbed the falling guard. "Idiot!" he snapped. "You women. Move off without running. You may be shot if you run. And shut up!"

That was appropriate because several had screamed in fright. "Skut. Take a child and get out of here," snapped his father.

They were nearly at the stairwell before someone started rattling the doors. A shot rang out. The armoured jump-troopers made a wall as the rest ducked and dived for the stairwell.

They pulled the last person down, and tumbled down the stairs. Above them, a few shots sounded.

The sergeant came bundling down. "Boat shed," snapped Podge's father. "They can lean over and shoot."

"Snarky!"

There was no answer.

Skut went cold, and turned back to the stair.

Here. It was pretty weak, but he nearly fell over with relief.

Food!

Skut managed a weak chuckle. "Where are you, you pest? I nearly died of fright."

Flew over edge of pier to catch a fish. No fish, too much rain. Flew to Podge. No food.

Skut ran up to his father, who put a hand on his shoulder. "If your mother knew..."

"But she doesn't, Papa. And Snarky got him. Snarky

needs food, Papa. Shocking someone uses a lot of his energy."

"There are bait freezers along the back wall."

Skut did his best to tell Snarky, and then ran, pushing his way through the crowd, up, into the huge boatshed, where the charter boats waited on their launch-rails. He found Podge, Snarky on his shoulder, trying to break open a box of bait. Skut grabbed it from him, and threw it with all his strength on the concrete floor so it broke, and then pried two small frozen fish apart with his knife and warmed the fragments between his palms—which Snarky was trying to drag out of his fingers and eat. Once he had fed him, the little storm-dragon squirreled into his shirt...and then said *wet!*

"Go sleep in Podge's shirt. He's dry."

There were people everywhere in among the boats. They were wetter and colder than he was, and were climbing up into the boats, and taking things from the lockers. A jump-trooper came running up, saying that Podge was wanted, so they both went.

His father was there, along with Podge's father. "They need more men," said his father. "I will be going to guide them."

"Papa, they could come in through the entrance to the boat shed. It's next to the other hotel, so it should be safe. Podge can open that door and these people can go out that way."

"That would be easier!" said the sergeant. "Any more smart ideas, boys?"

"Well," said Skut's father. "I am not like these boys, but there is the stair and the lift to the kitchens on the second floor. And then there are fire doors. We could open them, ja."

"Let's talk to the CO," said Podge's father. "Before these two get involved in any more military adventures and give me grey hairs. Your mothers both came with the troop carrier, along with the rest of them. Time you went. Out there, it was your world, Skut. In here, it's the soldiers' job. The Ghats don't know how to deal with Vann's World, but urban fighting is their thing."

As it worked out, they all went, along with a hundred and eighty-nine hostages. "There are going to be some happy people out there," the sergeant said. "Looks like they used the kids as leverage to keep the people who were supposed to make the place look normal when the Premier's ship landed, behaving themselves. So now they just have those still in the hotel."

It wasn't just the people who were glad to see their kids, Podge and Skut discovered. They were also popular. It was awkward being kissed by people who weren't your own mother, while Fred was proudly telling everyone that he had pulled Skut up. Snarky woke up and climbed out of Podge's shirt and onto Skut's shoulder and hissed at them. And all the girls said "Ah! So cute!" Skut was very glad to see his own mother waiting with the troop carrier at the door. He realised, then, that it wasn't just Snarky's batteries that were flat. He felt like he wanted to sleep for a week. And eat. He just wasn't too sure in which order.

EPILOGUE

It wasn't quite all over, of course. The Colonel got Podge down into the boat shed to hocus-pocus the locks and the lights that evening. The Ghats, they worked out, were down to twenty-three men, and still had some two hundred and ten hostages. It turned out there were security cameras in the lobby, dining rooms, and the bar and lounge—all the downstairs rooms, even the entertainment center that Jaccie and Hillary had been so fond of enjoying with their friends. It was possible to establish exactly where the guards were and weren't. They were thinly-stretched, especially as a number of the hostages had chosen the final escape of those left on the jetty—when their guards had rushed out of the rooms they were in, and with the chaos caused by the overhead sprinklers—to take advantage of the fire-doors and escape. A few people had been hurt in the panic, but almost all the hostages in the dining room and in the bar and lounge had escaped.

The Ghats had concentrated all the remaining hostages into the second dining room, because the rain and wind were now coming in the shot-out glass at the far end of the lobby. They set themselves up in the catering kitchen, which had a hatch to the dining hall where they could watch the hostages and remain far more protected. Besides, there was food and drink available to them there.

The Ghats didn't have night-vision gear, and they were unaware that a door at the back of the kitchen led to the main kitchens—to which the jump-troops had access thanks to the boat house lift and stairs. They found out their error when they were suddenly plunged into darkness and the flash-bangs rolled in.

That only left the six Ghats who were guarding the lobby and keeping a lookout over the jetty and the street. They, as the sergeant said when asked, didn't have hostages for anyone to worry about.

That had left them down to Commander Ishmaeli, his lieutenant and three soldiers, and the General Manager and her Hotel Manager husband, plus their daughter, in the penthouse suite. The Commander called for negotiations about his three valuable hostages before the jump-troopers had found him—they'd been checking the hotel for hide-aways by the method of opening or knocking a hole in each door and tossing a flash-bang in before checking if anyone was inside. Skut thought it sounded like fun, when the sergeant told him about it. He, Podge, and Snarky found they'd been sort of adopted by the jump-troops.

The only flaw to Commander Ishmaeli's strategy was that, among the hostages which had been freed, was one person who hadn't been living in the settlement. He was the auditor, who along with the new administrator had come to Vann's World to fire the GM and most of the staff, and take over the running of the Council. They had just been informing the GM of this, when Commander Ishmaeli had walked in. When the new Administrator demanded to know what he was doing there... Ishmaeli shot the new Administrator. The auditor had been tied up, tossed in a cupboard, and later transported to the hotel, where the Hotel Manager—the GM's husband—had kept him prisoner in his suite until the Ghat takeover.

The auditor had insisted on being taken to see the Colonel.

Podge's father had been there, and had relayed what he'd said: "They have embezzled millions from the state. Monies paid for distribution to the displaced farmers for their maintenance was supposed to be disbursed by them. The displaced were supposed to be housed in the hotels, seeing as they were not in use, and that money too was appropriated, and instead they collected rentals from them!" At this point the auditor managed a thin-lipped smile. "They thought they'd transferred their funds out of our reach, but the transaction was flagged and the monies seized. It will be reimbursed to the injured parties over the next few months. But those two are hand-in-glove with the Emir of Ghatistan's agents. I demand, Sir, that you arrest them!"

Given that information, Colonel Morgan felt waiting for the negotiating team was un-necessary, and they had a choice of surrender or die. They chose wisely.

By the next day, when the negotiating team finally

arrived, the military were ready to leave. Colonel Morgan called them all in. "There'll be official enquiries and commissions and all sorts," he said, apologetically. "But the Ghats are going to be hurt and embarrassed by all of this—the ringleaders are singing already. The Confederated Worlds owe you a debt of gratitude. I'll try and see that some of it is repaid, but, well, you know, governments... In the meantime, I'm leaving a garrison of twenty men here, while the Ghat ship is being searched for from orbit. Not that I think that the ship or its crew will cause trouble, but it will remain a military situation until they're dealt with. I've revived your old commission, Captain Greene, whether you like it or not. You're in charge of them, and you're the military administrator of this settlement. The auditor informs me you're the only Council employee with wholly clean hands—though in the fashion of bean-counters everywhere, he is having fits about the use and destruction of Council machinery. I have, I think been able to prevail on him that these were destroyed by the Ghats, and he should send them an invoice."

Colonel Morgan stuck out his hand. "Now, I would like to shake you all by the hand, and remove myself from this planet, before my men have to deal with any more of the wildlife or the wild weather, and I have to know what you're up to. Good luck straightening it all out."

"Well," said Podge when, like most of settlement they'd seen the ship off. "School is closed for two weeks. It'll be a bit dull going back to it."

"It'll be different," said Skut. "I'm allowed to take Snarky. Bargen's had a nervous breakdown...and the parents voted to make Crawf the new head, after what he did on the jetty. He told me I'm allowed to take Snarky, provided I...or rather, we...don't disrupt classes!"

That was enough to make Podge laugh himself into falling over, and to get dive bombed by Snarky, who thought it a great game.

Fun! said Snarky.

PLEASE, TIP YOUR AUTHORS!

At Raconteur Press, our motto is *Have Fun, Get Paid!* Hopefully you enjoyed the stories in this volume. If you did, please take the time to leave a quick review. Our authors love to hear that people enjoyed their stories and it encourages them to write more like them.

If you liked a story by a particular author, go ahead and find, then follow their author page. This enables you to get notifications about their next release.

To follow Raconteur Press, which you should totally do, subscribe to our Substack at https://raconteurpress.substack.com/ and you'll be amused by updates from Farnsworth the editing orc, notified of any new releases, and for the low price of free, get special content seen nowhere else.